Animal Roll Call

Violin 2 — Mary Cohen

Space Attack

Violin 2

Robert Spearing

March-like, energetic and sinister ♩ = 120–156

Violin 2

Alone on the Lake

Robert Spearing

Very gentle ♩ = 112

pp sempre

Violin 2

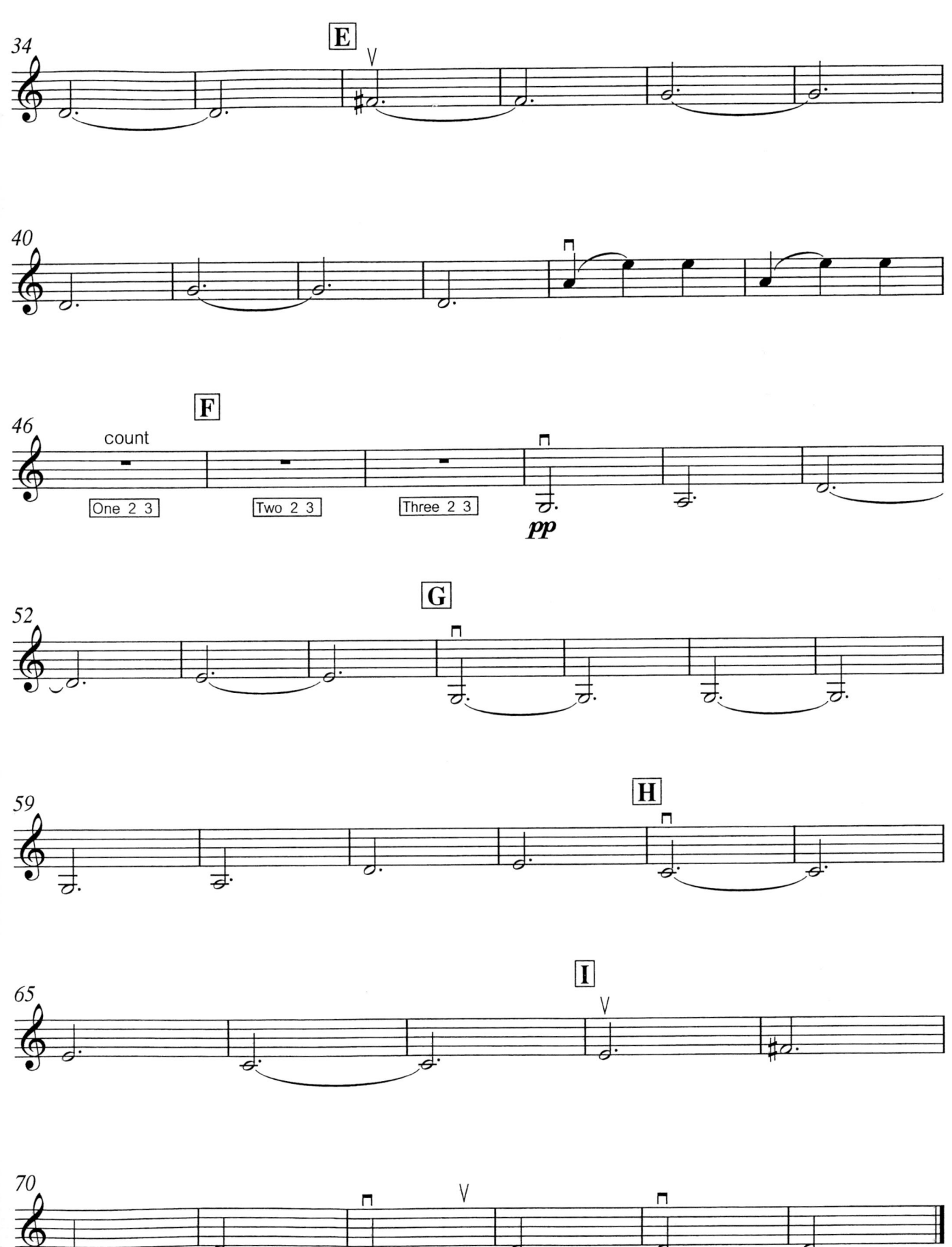

Animal Roll Call

Mary Cohen

Space Attack

Viola

Robert Spearin

March-like, energetic and sinister ♩ = 120 –156

Alone on the Lake

Robert Spearing

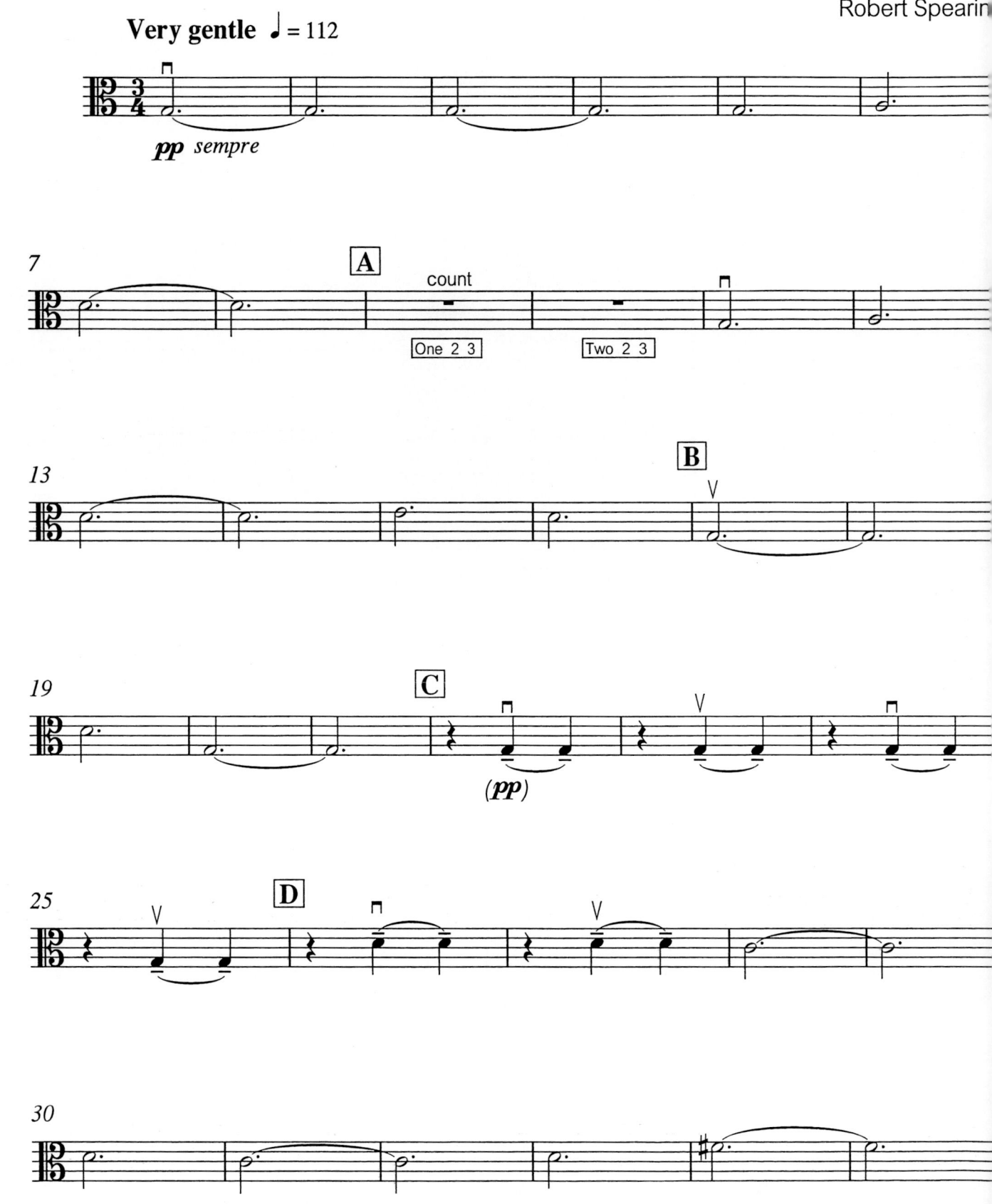

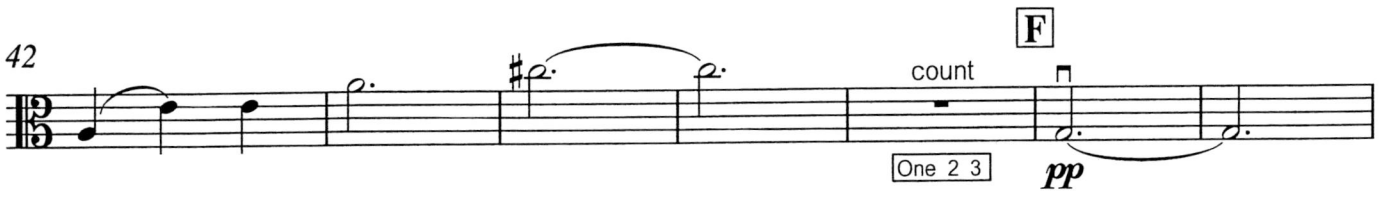

Chinese Street Festival
Drums and Dragons

Mary Cohen

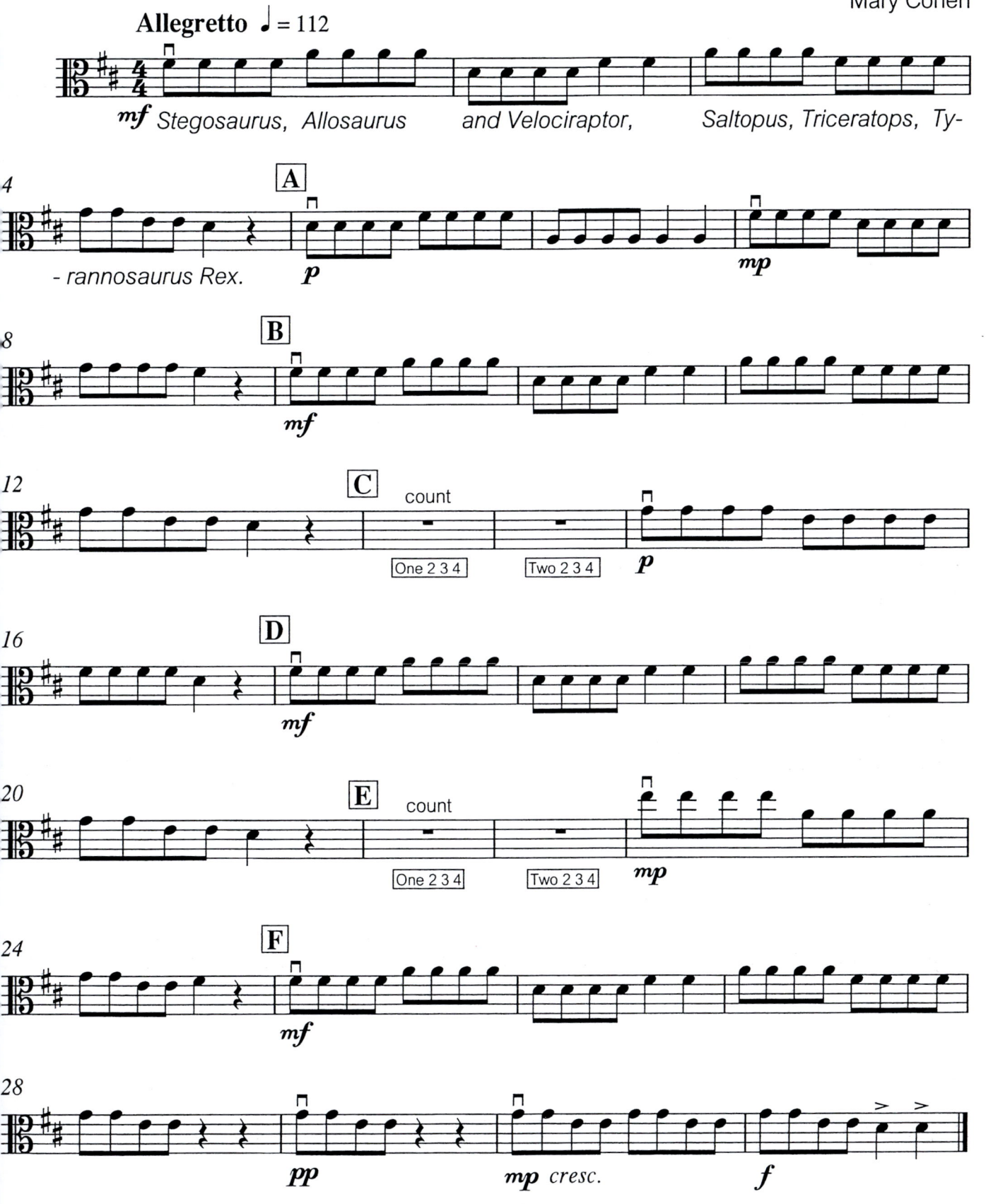

What the Dinos saw

Mary Cohen

What the Dinos saw

Violin 3

Mary Cohen

Violin 3

Animal Roll Call

Mary Cohen

Space Attack

Violin 3

Robert Spearin

March-like, energetic and sinister ♩ = 120 –156

Alone on the Lake

Violin 3

Robert Spearin

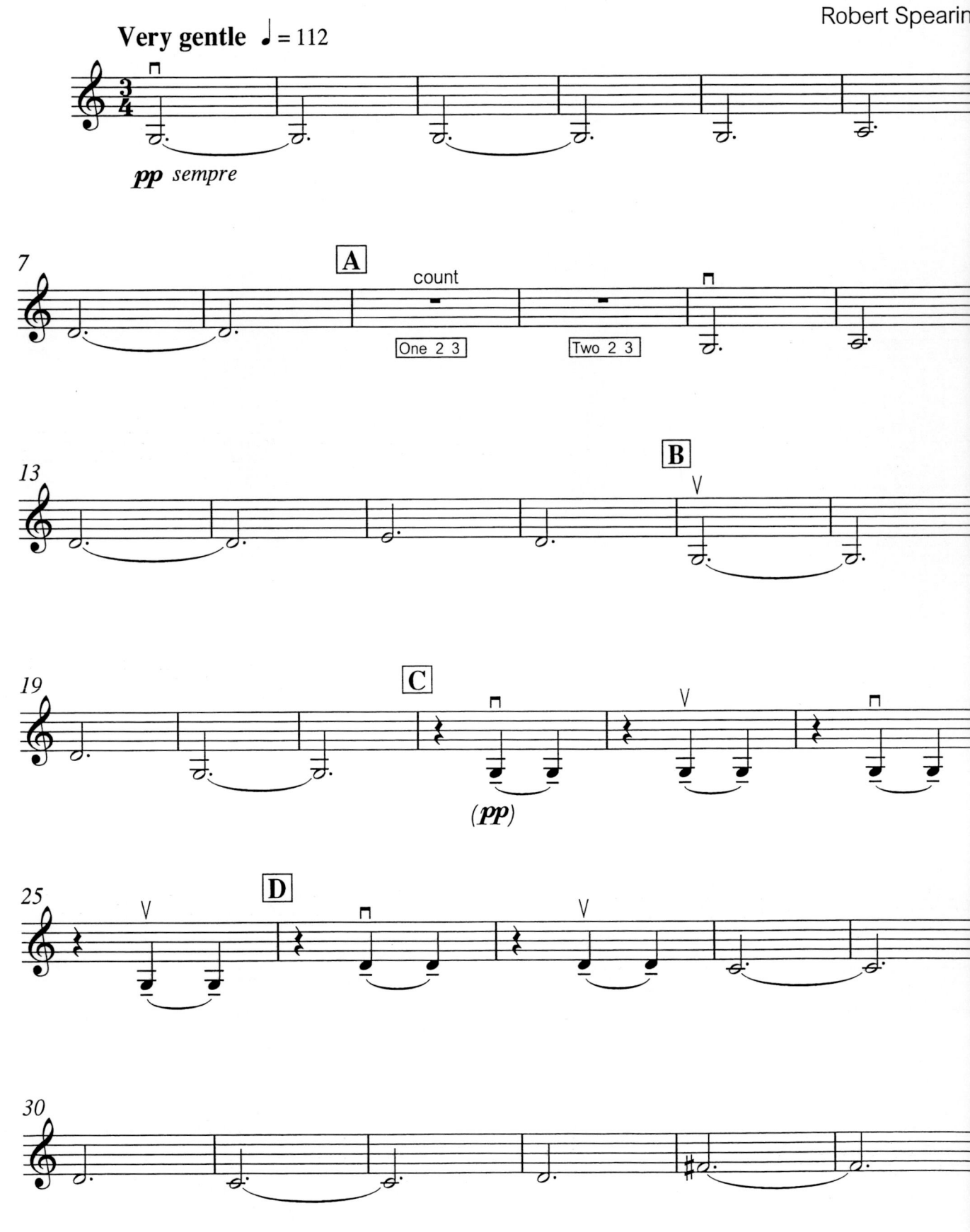

Violin 3

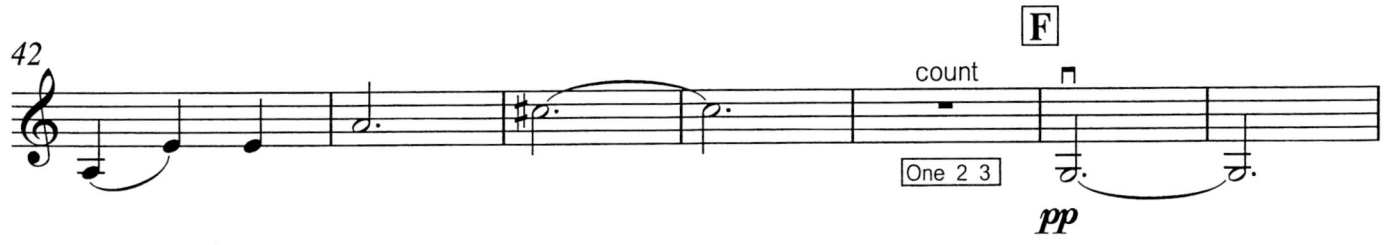

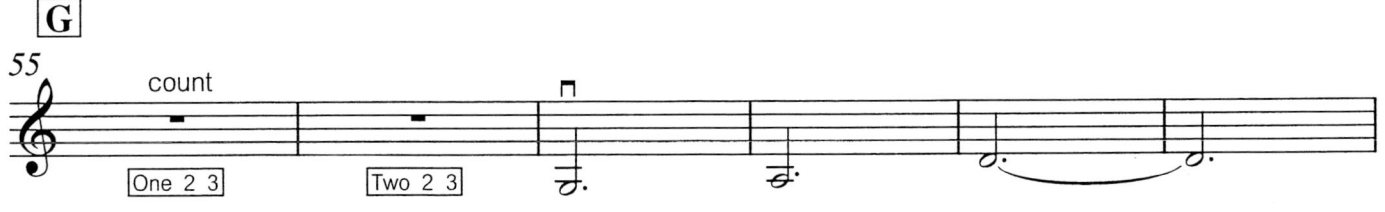

Animal Roll Call

Mary Cohen

Space Attack

Cello

Robert Spearin

March-like, energetic and sinister ♩ = 120–156

Alone on the Lake

Robert Speari

What the Dinos saw

Mary Cohen

Animal Roll Call

Mary Cohen

Vivace ♪ = 144 – 208

mf Elephant Alligator Hippopotamus

sim.

Space Attack

Violin 1

Robert Spearin

March-like, energetic and sinister ♩ = 120 –156

CODA
37
count
One 2 3 4
pp
H
43
I
count
One 2 3 4
J
49
mf
K
ff
54
sul pont.
nat.
f
L
59
M
mp
cresc.
64
ff
N
count
One 2 3 4
68
ff
count
One 2 3 4
Two 2 3 4
ppp

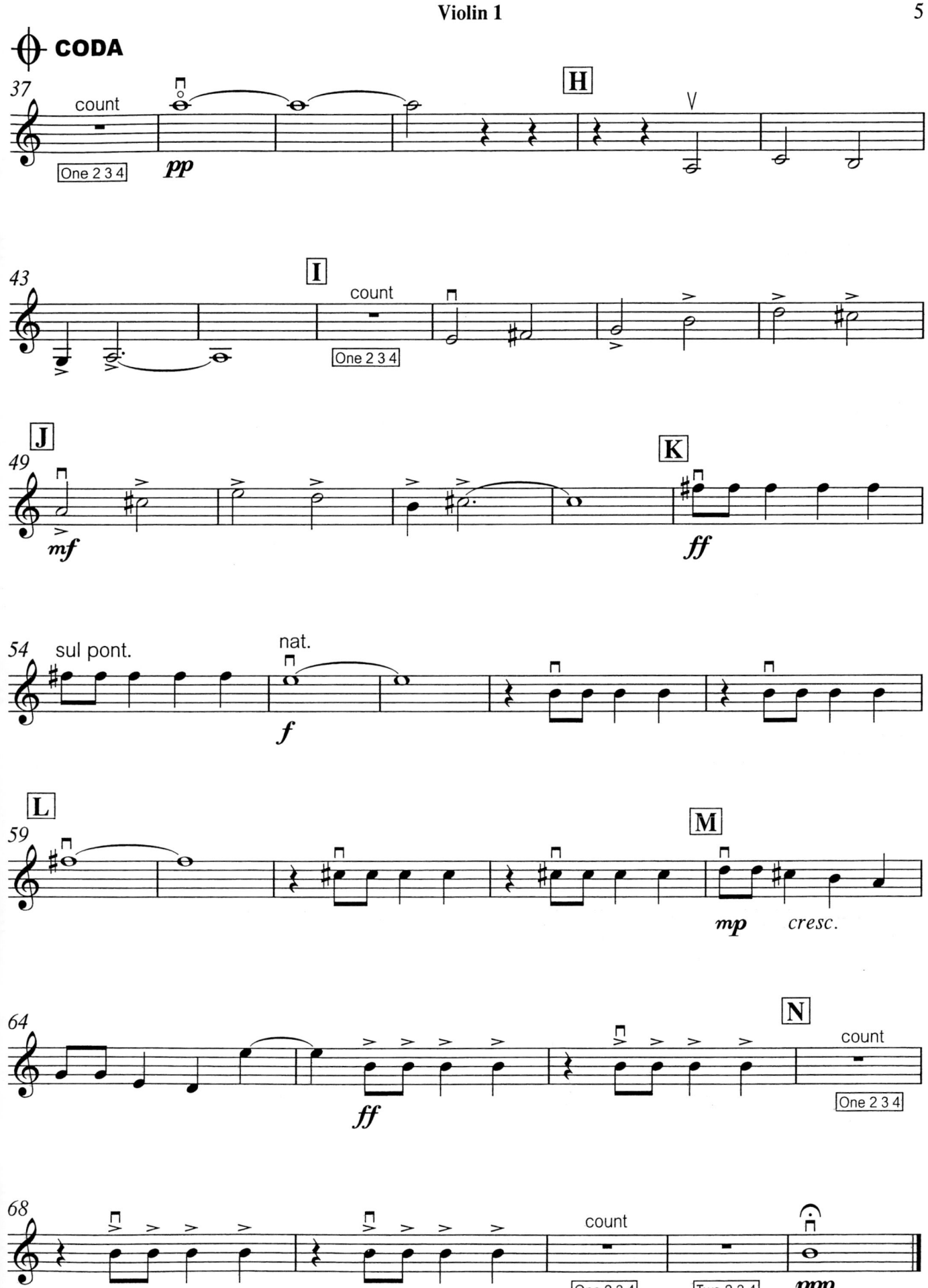

Alone on the Lake

Robert Spearing

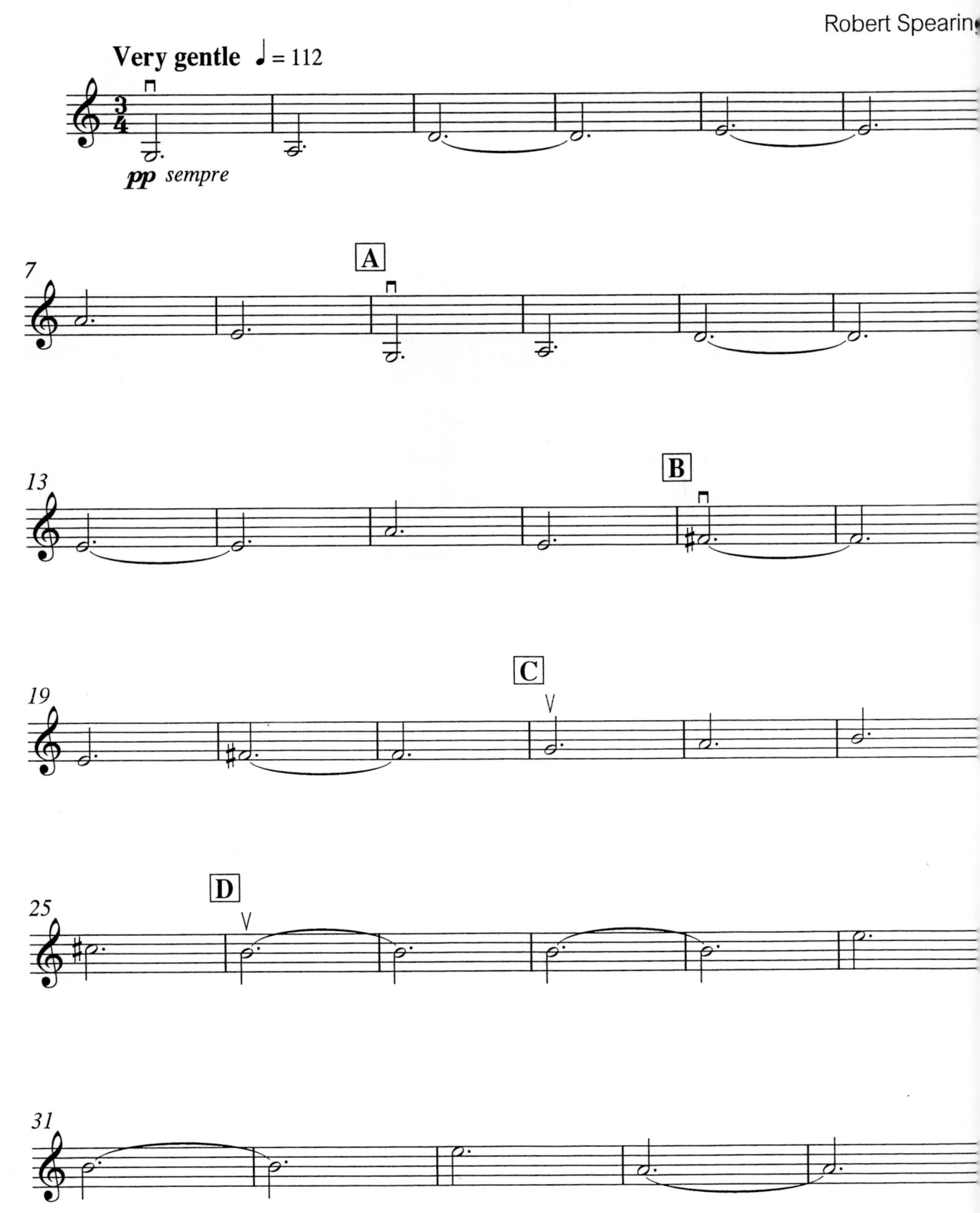

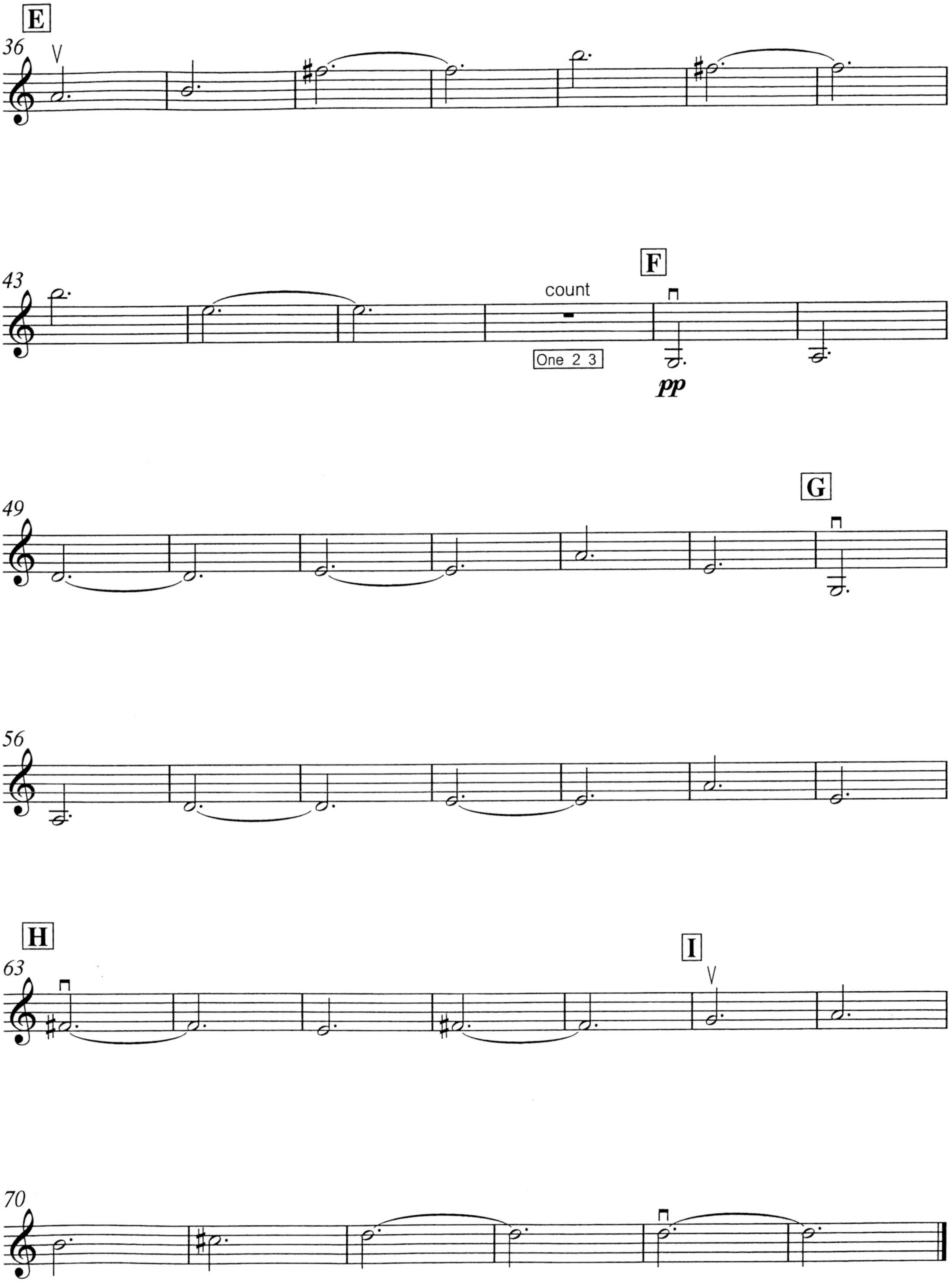
E
36
43
count
F
One 2 3
pp
49
G
56
H
63
I
70

Chinese Street Festival
Drums and Dragons

Mary Cohen

Andantino ♩ = 104

Rondosaurus

**Stegosaurus, Allosaurus and Velociraptor,
Saltopus, Triceratops, Tyrannosaurus Rex.**

Mary Cohen

What the Dinos saw

Violin 1

Mary Cohen

Mary Cohen & Robert Spearing

Quartet start
Level 1

Original repertoire for beginner string quartets

© 1998 by Faber Music Ltd
First published in 1999 by Faber Music Ltd
3 Queen Square London WC1N 3AU
Cover design by S & M Tucker
Music processed by Mary Cohen and Jackie Leigh
Printed in England by Caligraving Ltd
All rights reserved

ISBN 0-571-51881-8

To buy Faber Music publications or to find out about the full range of titles available please contact your local retailer or Faber Music sales enquiries:

Faber Music Ltd, Burnt Mill, Elizabeth Way, Harlow CM20 2HX
Tel: +44 (0)1279 82 89 82   Fax: +44 (0)1279 82 89 83
sales@fabermusic.com   fabermusic.com

FABER ff MUSIC

Contents

	Score	All parts
Rondosaurus (Cohen)	3	1
What the Dinos saw (Cohen)	6	2
Animal Roll Call (Cohen)	9	3
Space Attack (Spearing)	12	4
Alone on the Lake (Spearing)	18	6
Chinese Street Festival (Cohen)	22	8

To the teacher

Quartetstart Level 1 has been designed as a first string quartet experience for young players whose individual standard is about grade (AB) 1-2. Apart from occasional one octave harmonics, the material throughout the book is written entirely in first finger pattern (0 1 23 4) in all parts, enabling the group to concentrate on the development of musical and ensemble skills. There is a simple strong rhythmic context to each piece, especially in 'Rondosaurus', 'Chinese Street Festival' and 'Animal Roll Call', where there is frequent rhythmic unison. To aid counting and to encourage players to make confident entries, multiple bars rest are written out with 'One 2 3 4, Two 2 3 4', etc. being added.

Mary Cohen

recommended
mixed duet experience, e.g. *Superduets 1* and *2* for violin and cello, published by Faber Music Ltd.

Rondosaurus

**Stegosaurus, Allosaurus and Velociraptor,
Saltopus, Triceratops, Tyrannosaurus Rex.**

Mary Cohen

REHEARSAL TIPS: The list of dinosaur names fits the rhythm of each set of four bars.
Encourage the players to count the bars rest out loud until all the entries are confident.

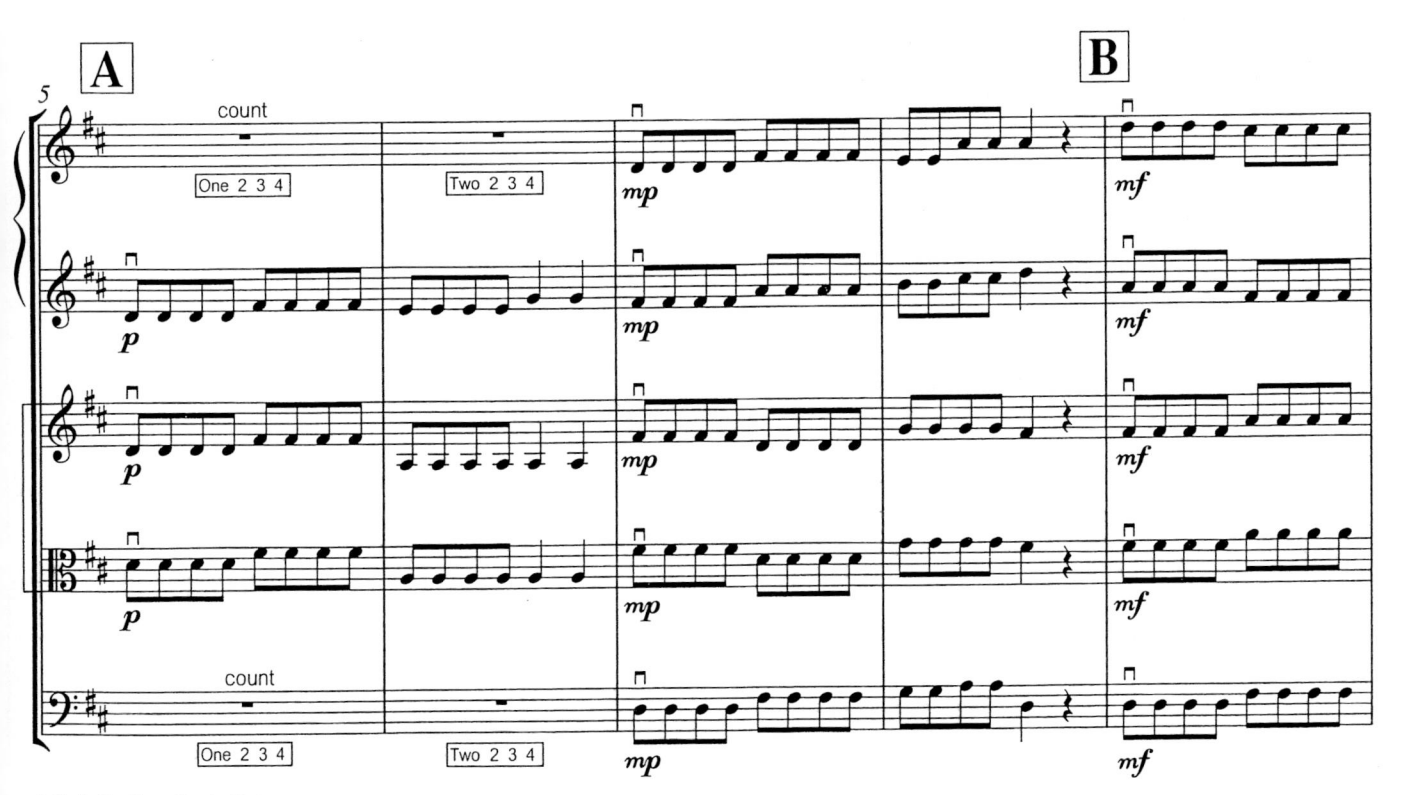

*Violin 3: alternative to Viola

© 1998 by Faber Music Ltd.

This music is copyright. Photocopying is illegal.

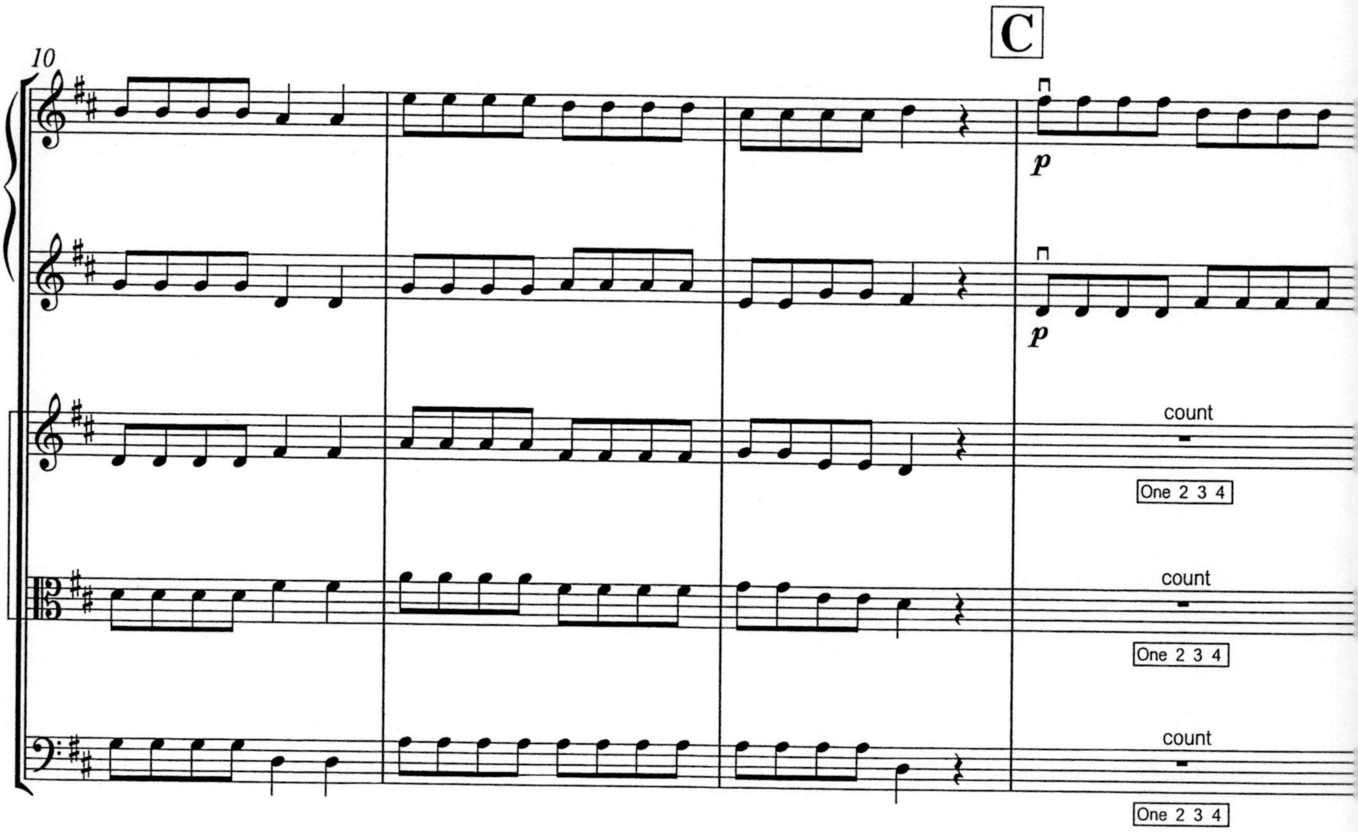
10
C
p
p
count
One 2 3 4
count
One 2 3 4
count
One 2 3 4

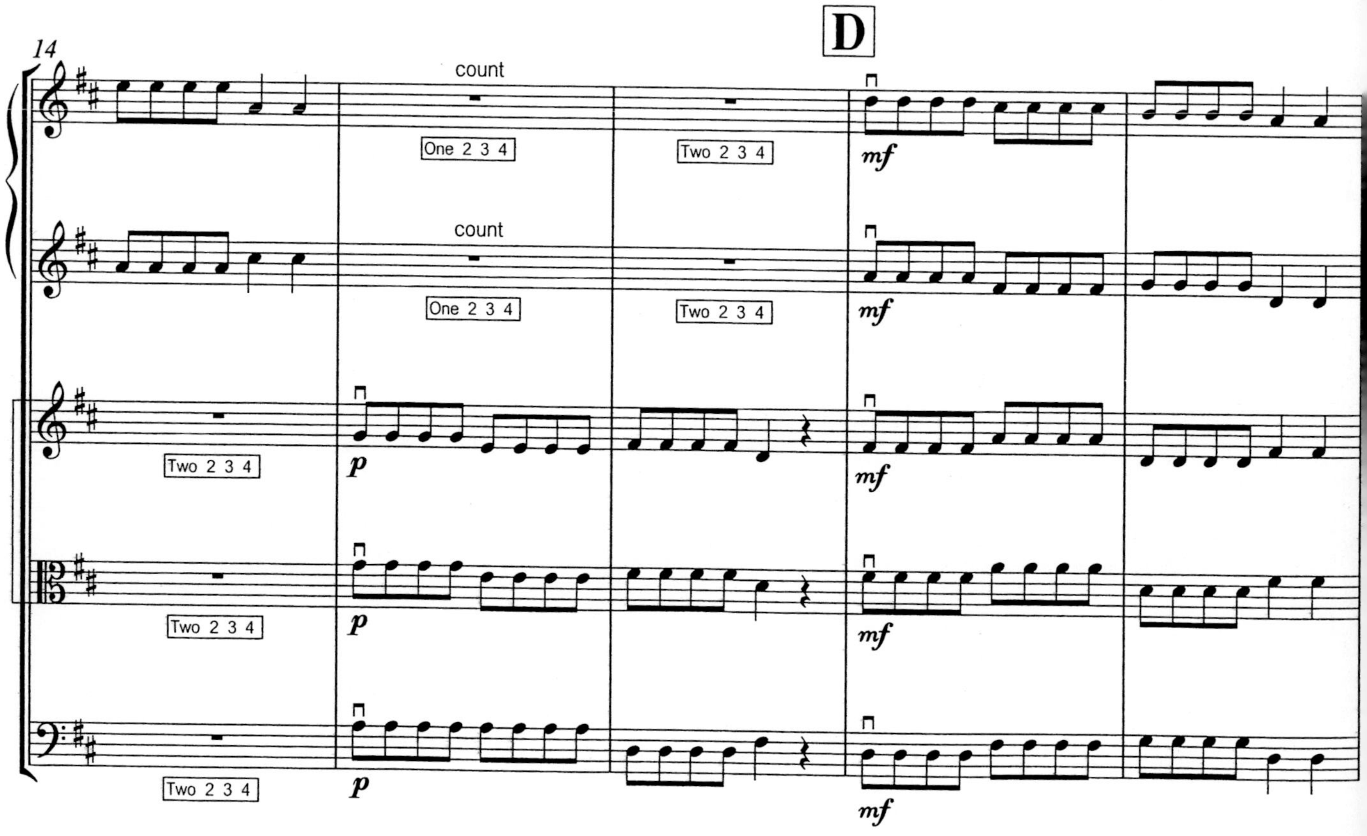
14
D
count
One 2 3 4
Two 2 3 4
mf
count
One 2 3 4
Two 2 3 4
mf
Two 2 3 4
p
mf
Two 2 3 4
p
mf
Two 2 3 4
p
mf

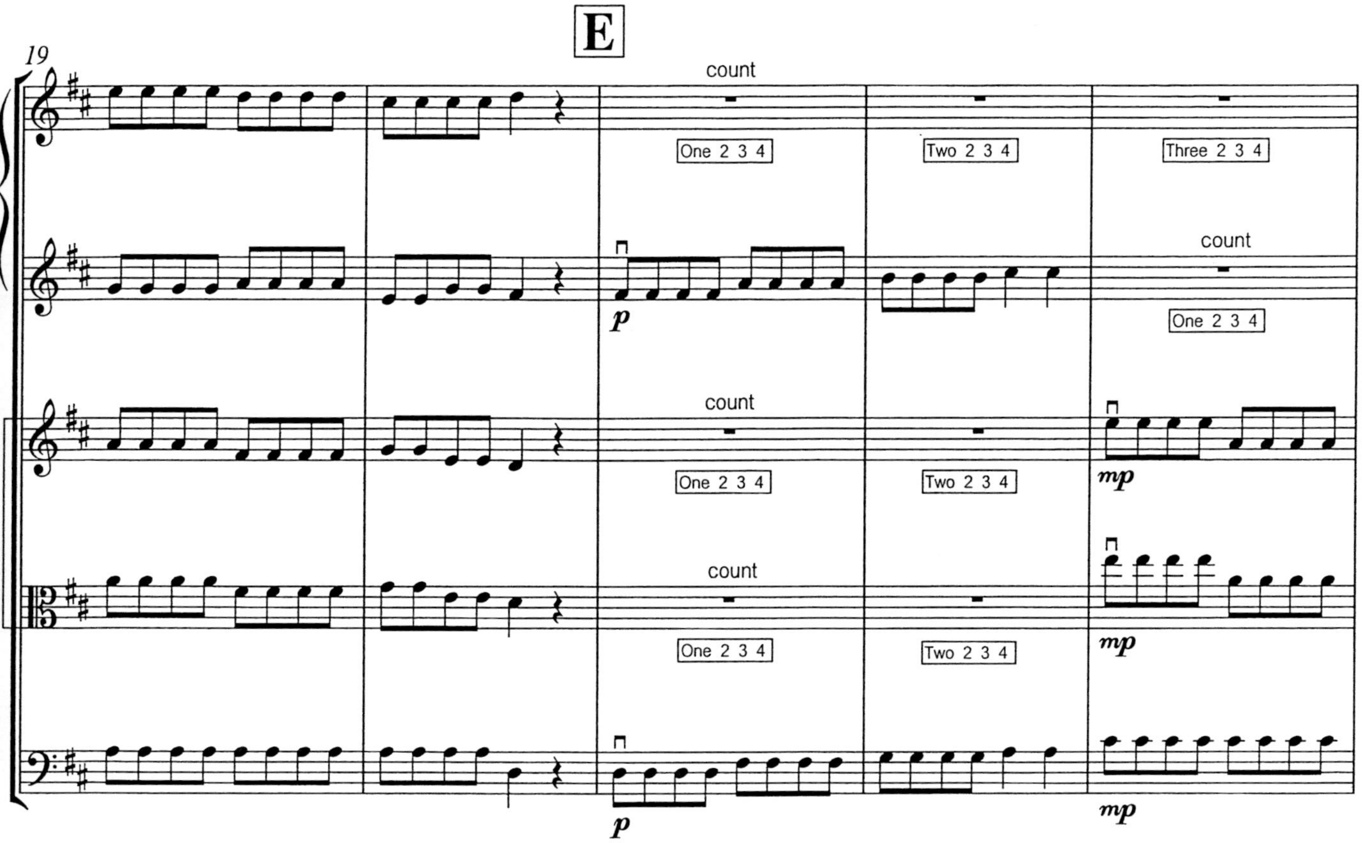
E
19
count
One 2 3 4
Two 2 3 4
Three 2 3 4
p
count
One 2 3 4
count
One 2 3 4
Two 2 3 4
mp
count
One 2 3 4
Two 2 3 4
mp
p
mp

F
24
mp
mf
mp
mf
mf
mf
mf

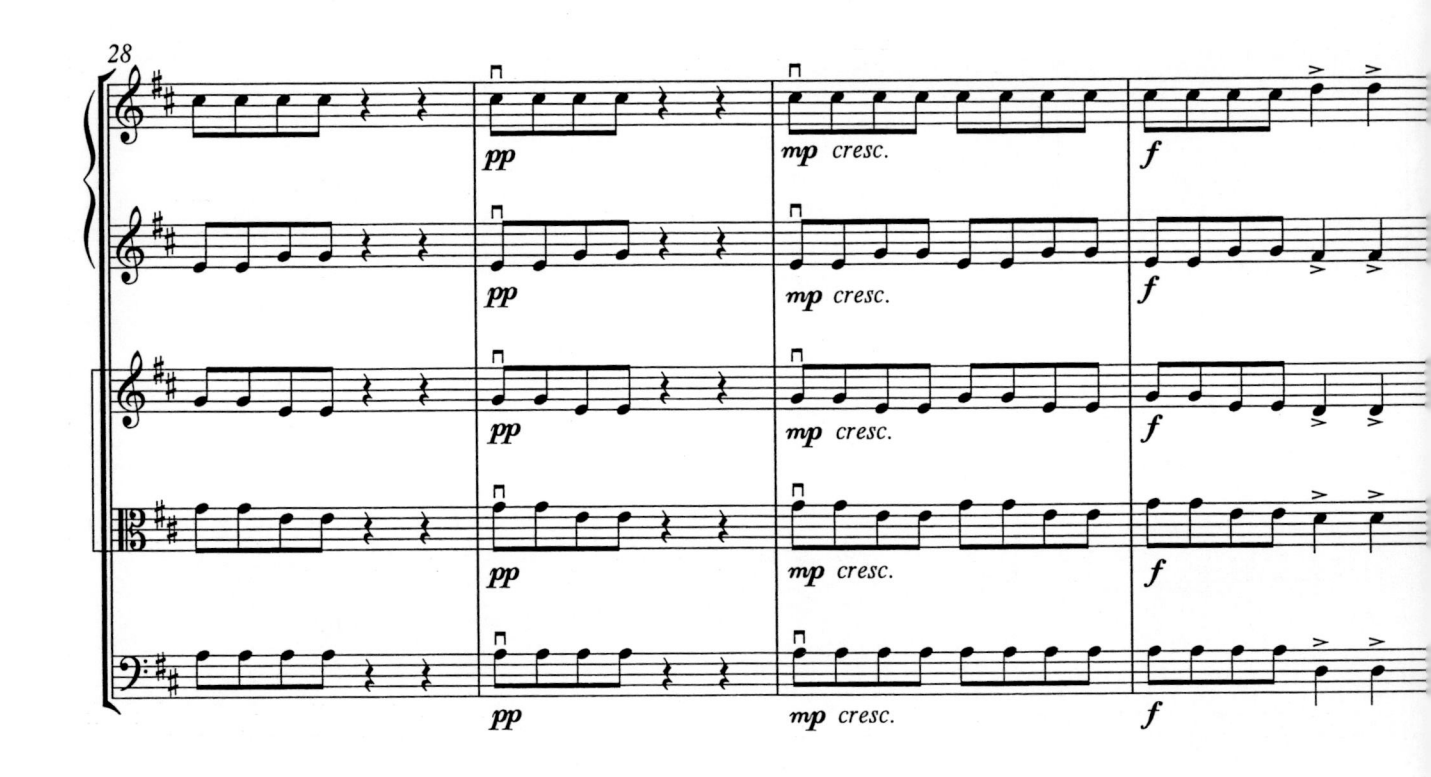

What the Dinos saw

Mary Cohen

REHEARSAL TIPS: Work at the sections B – E, G – I first (this is what the Dinos saw). Next add to these sections the 'build up' bars A – B and F – G. Finally tackle the first 4 bars and E – F (the Dinos' 'theme tune') and from I to the end.

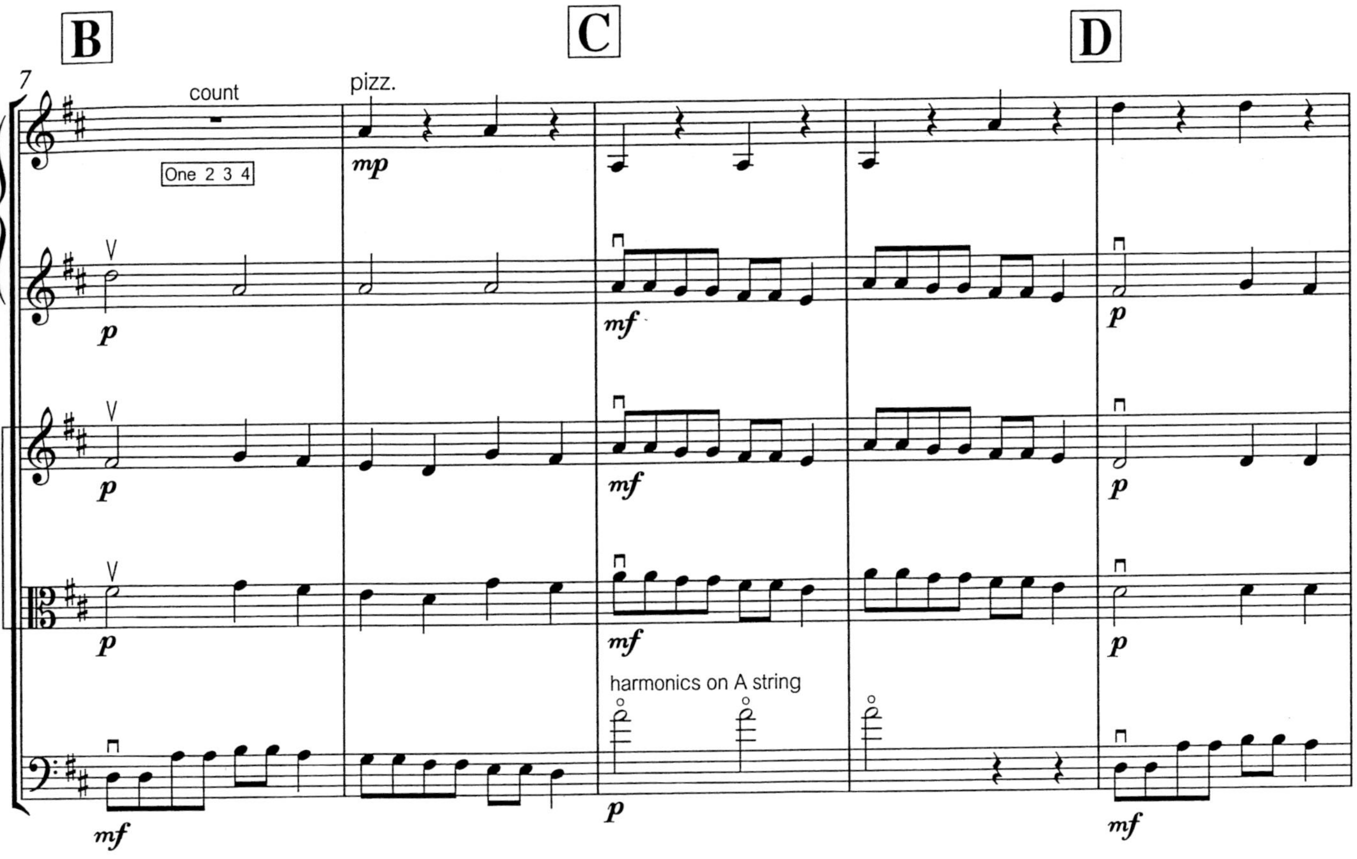
B
C
D
7
count
One 2 3 4
pizz.
mp
p
mf
harmonics on A string

E
F
12
arco
tremolo
near point
pizz.
count
One 2 3 4
Two 2 3 4
p
mf
pp

G
H
18
mp
mf
harmonics
count
One 2 3 4
Two 2 3 4
p
p sempre

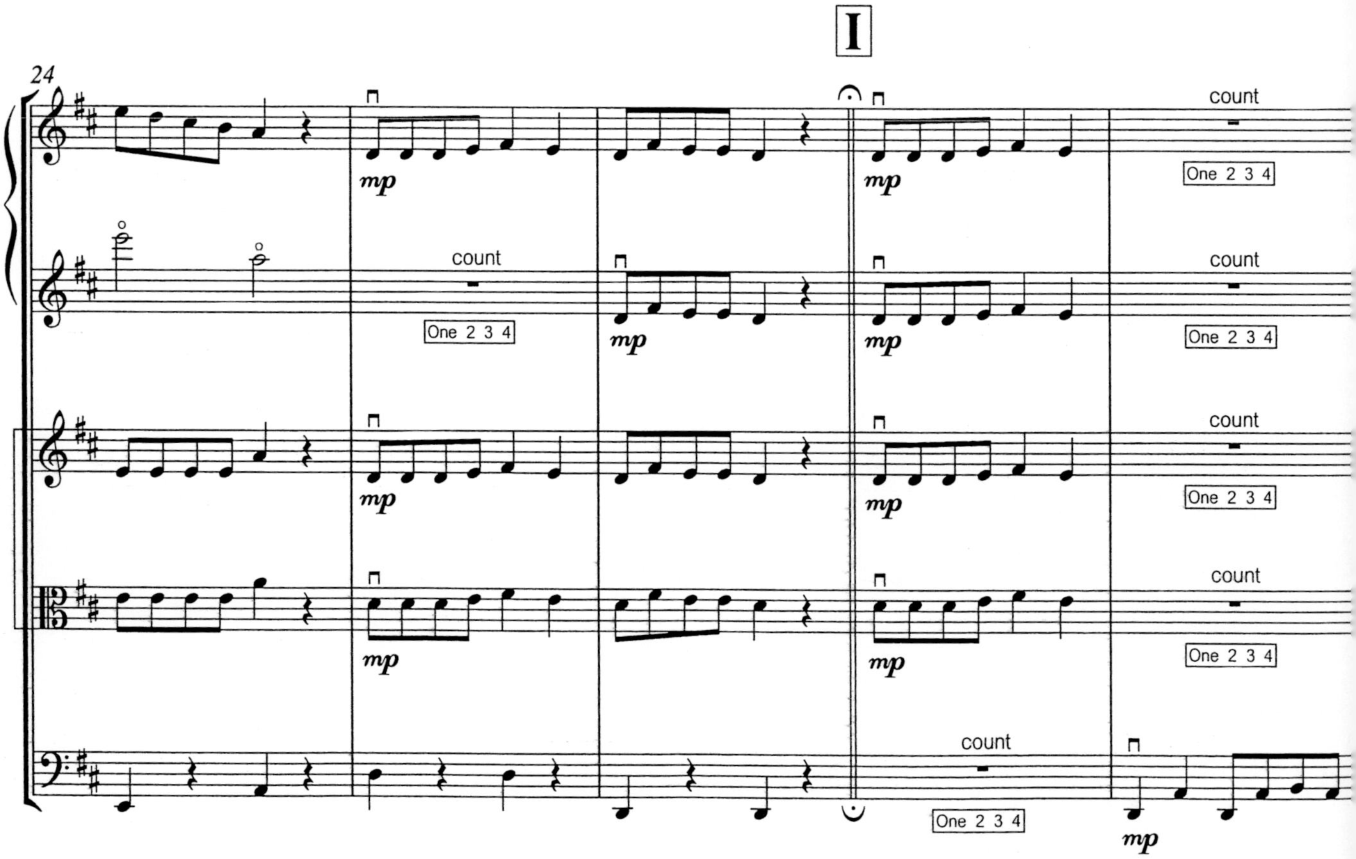
I
24
count
One 2 3 4
mp

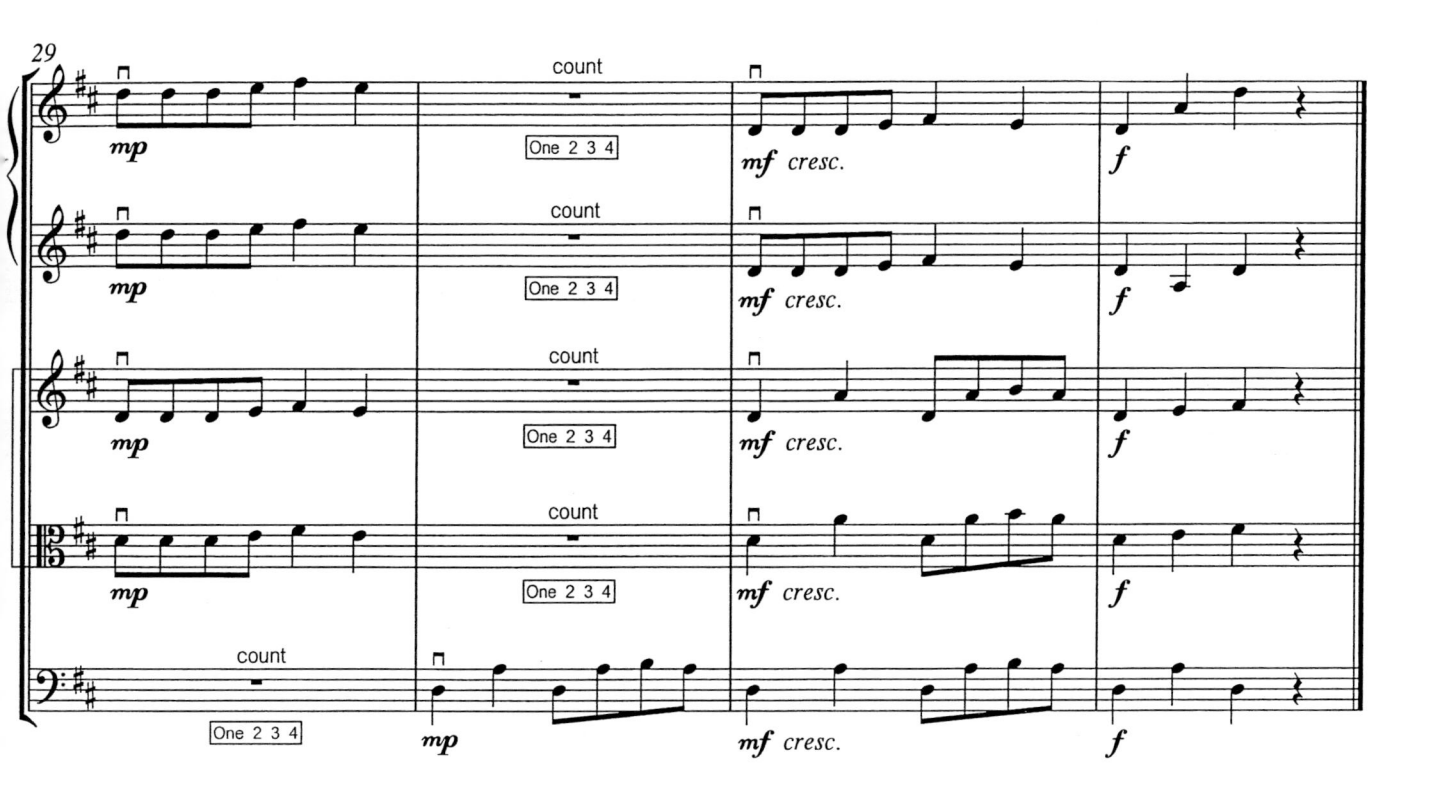

Animal Roll Call

Mary Cohen

REHEARSAL TIP: Before playing, read through the piece out loud, using the correct animal names: each one belongs to a different time signature!

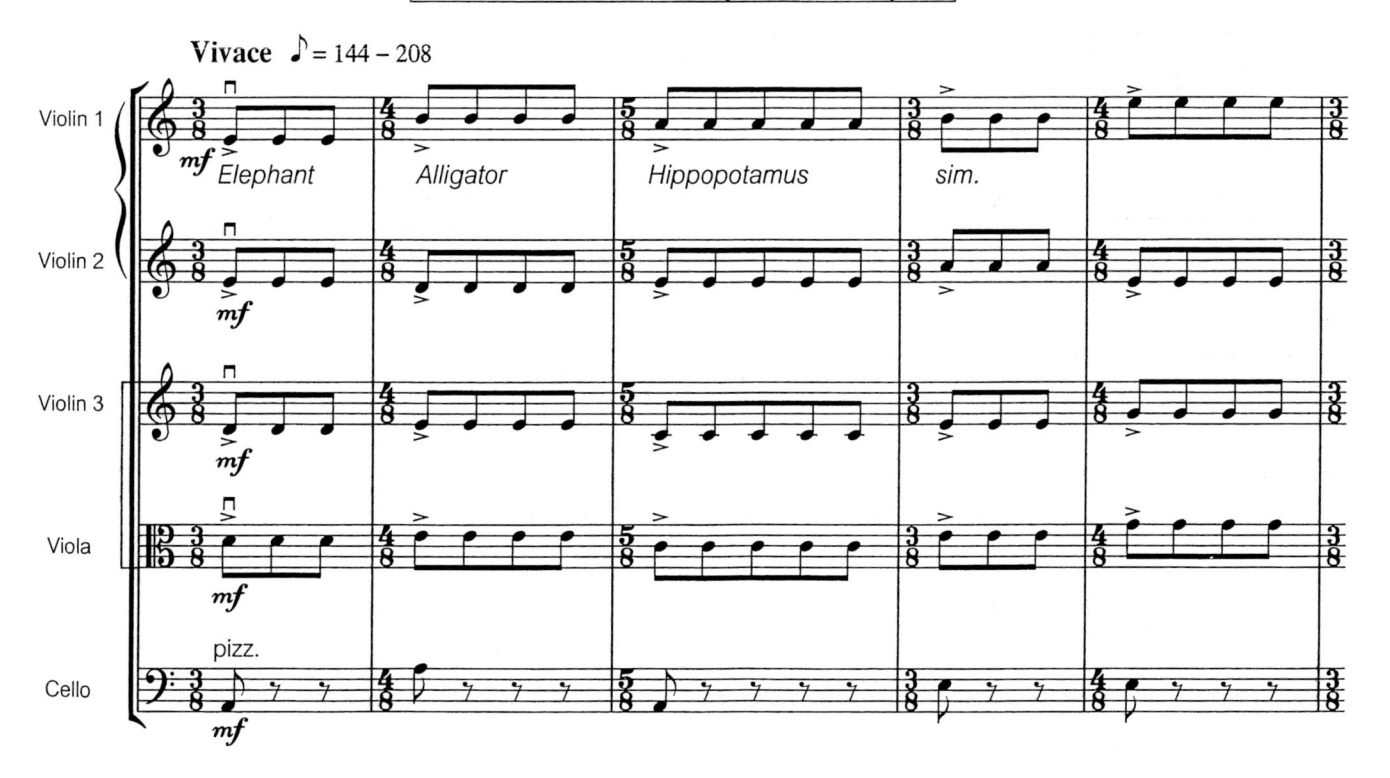

Vivace ♪ = 144 – 208

Elephant   Alligator   Hippopotamus   sim.

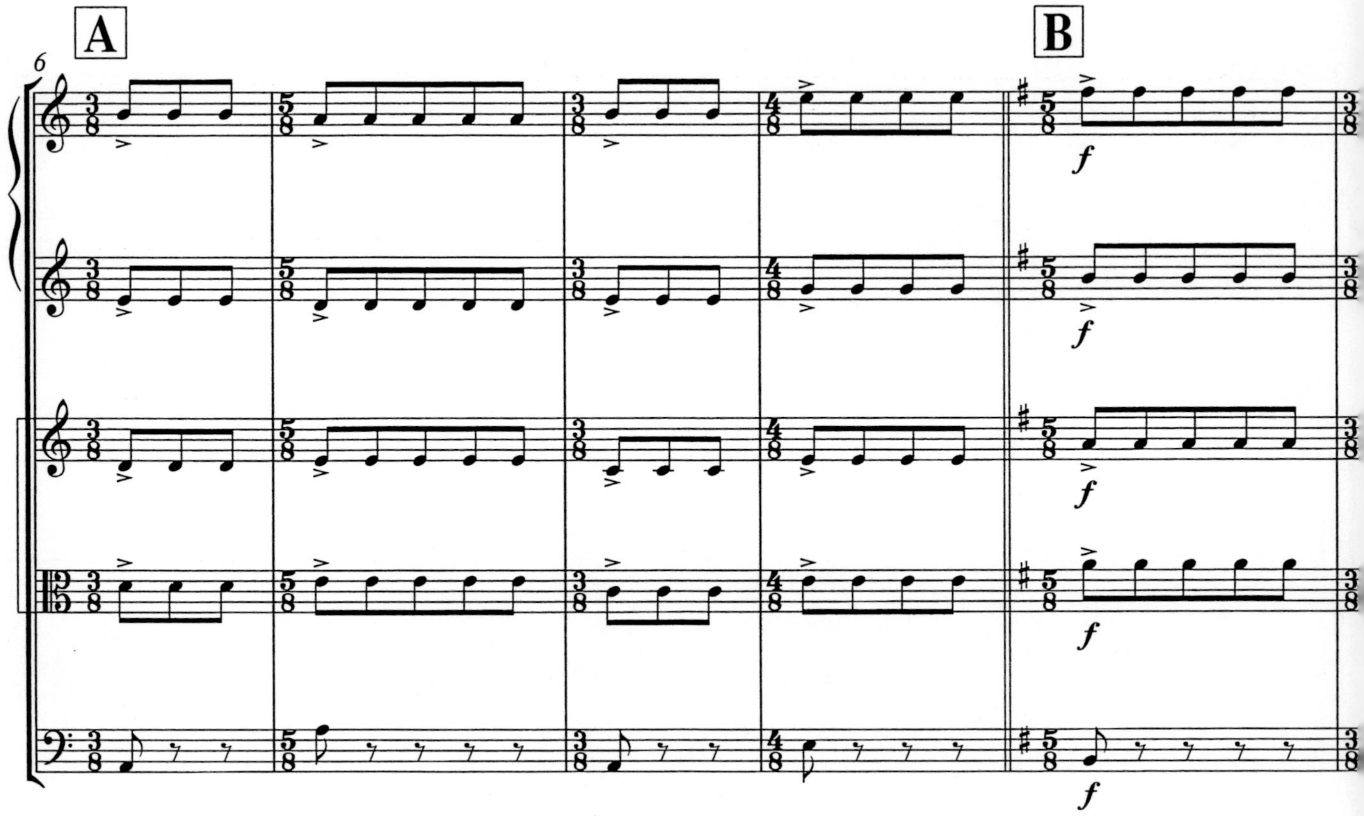
A
B
6
f
f
f
f
f

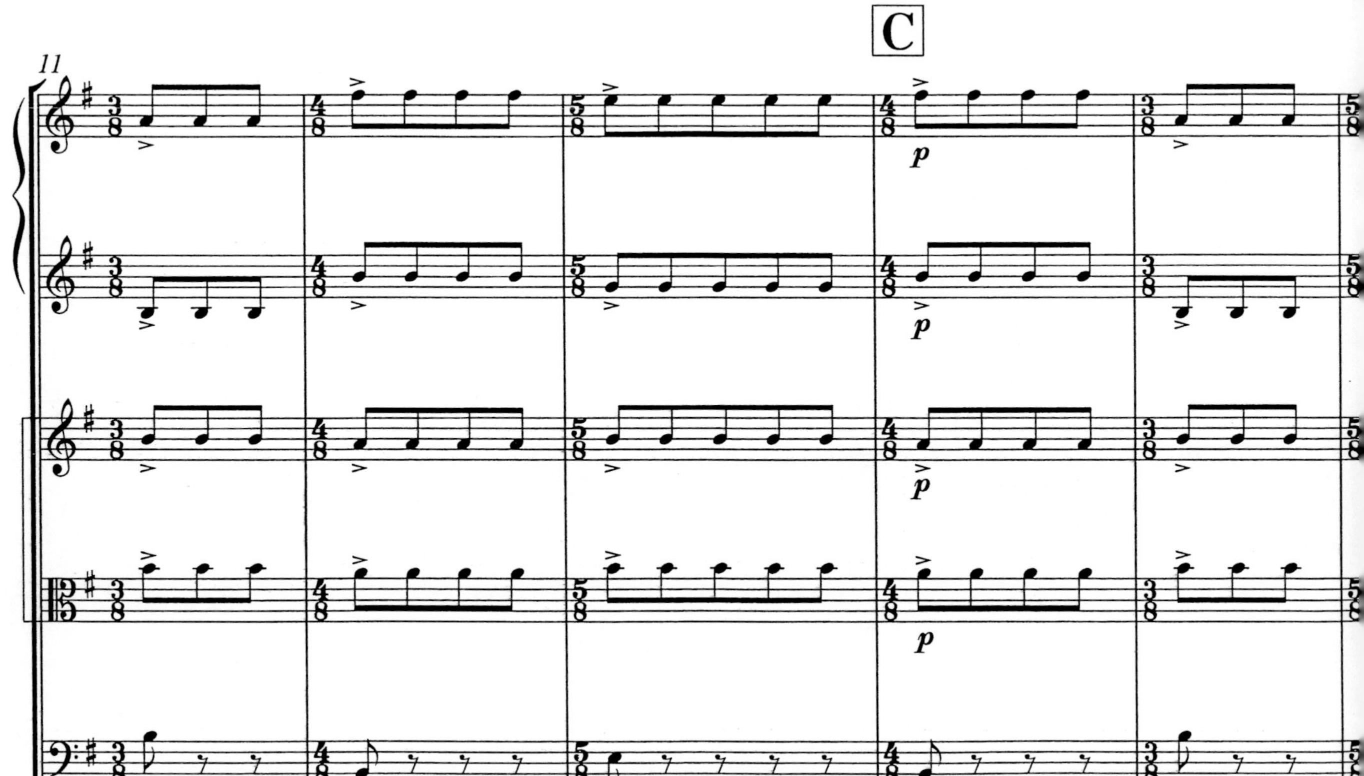
C
11
p
p
p
p
p

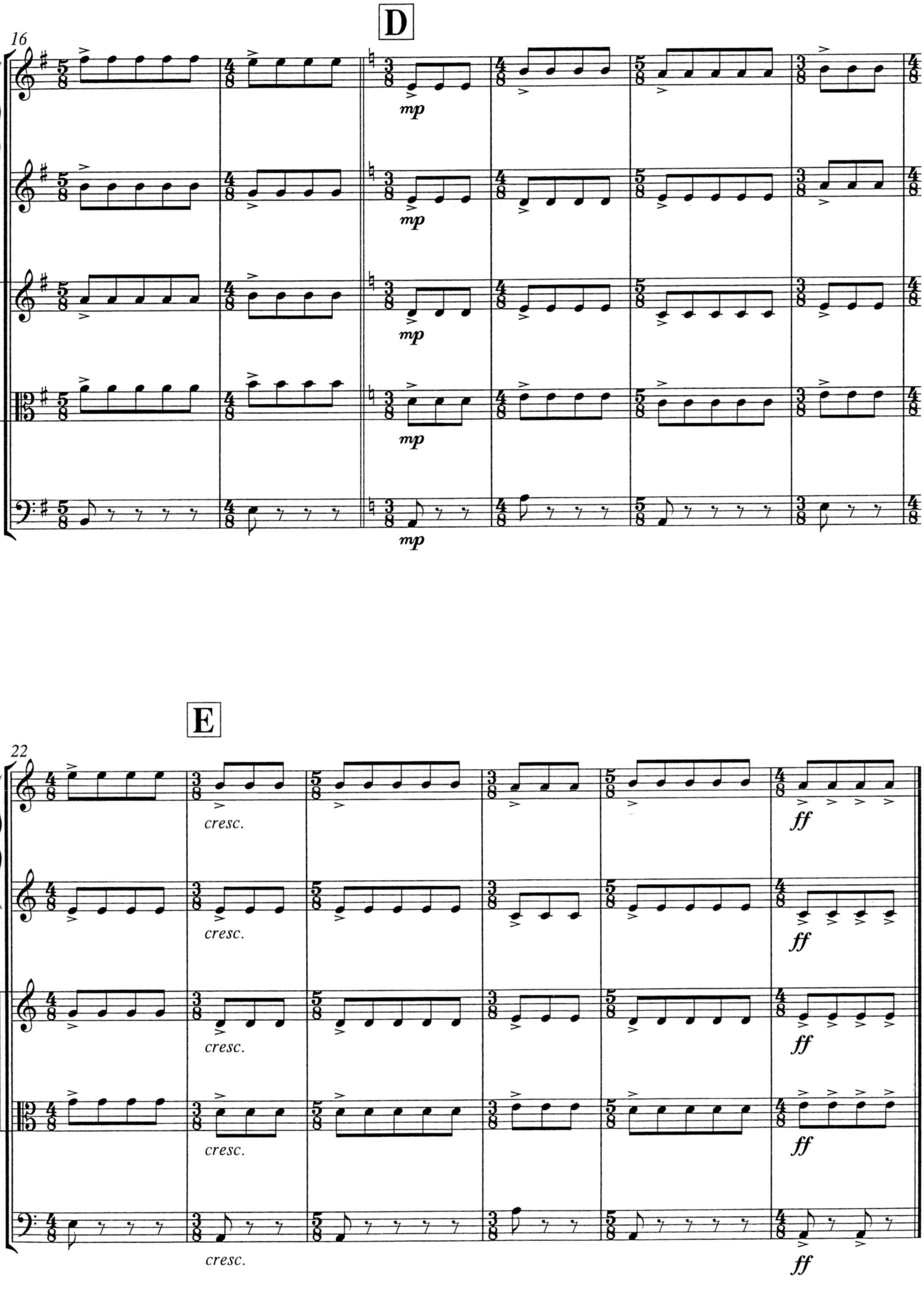
D
mp
mp
mp
mp
mp
E
cresc.
cresc.
cresc.
cresc.
cresc.
ff
ff
ff
ff
ff

Space Attack

Robert Spearing

REHEARSAL TIP: Accent the first of each pair of quavers/eighth notes when they are on the first beat of the bar but not when they follow a crotchet/quarter note rest.

C
13
ff
dim.
pp
f dim.
D
E
19
count
One 2 3 4
p
pp cresc.
pp sempre
cresc.
mp
p cresc.
4

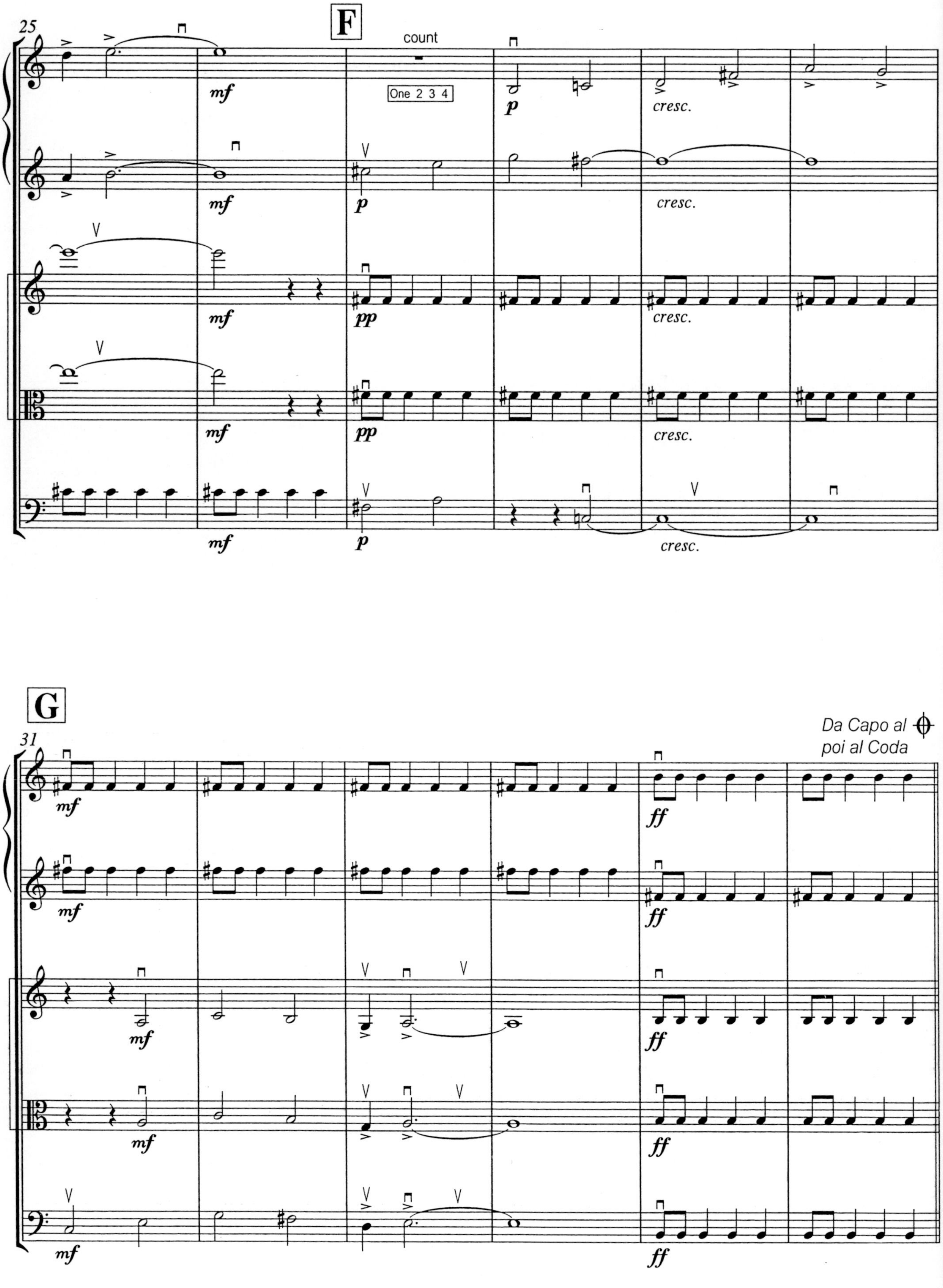
25
F
count
One 2 3 4
mf
p
pp
cresc.
G
31
Da Capo al
poi al Coda
mf
ff

CODA
37
count
One 2 3 4
pp
mp
H
count
One 2 3 4
count
One 2 3 4
pp
42
I
count
One 2 3 4
pp
pp
p
p
p
cresc.

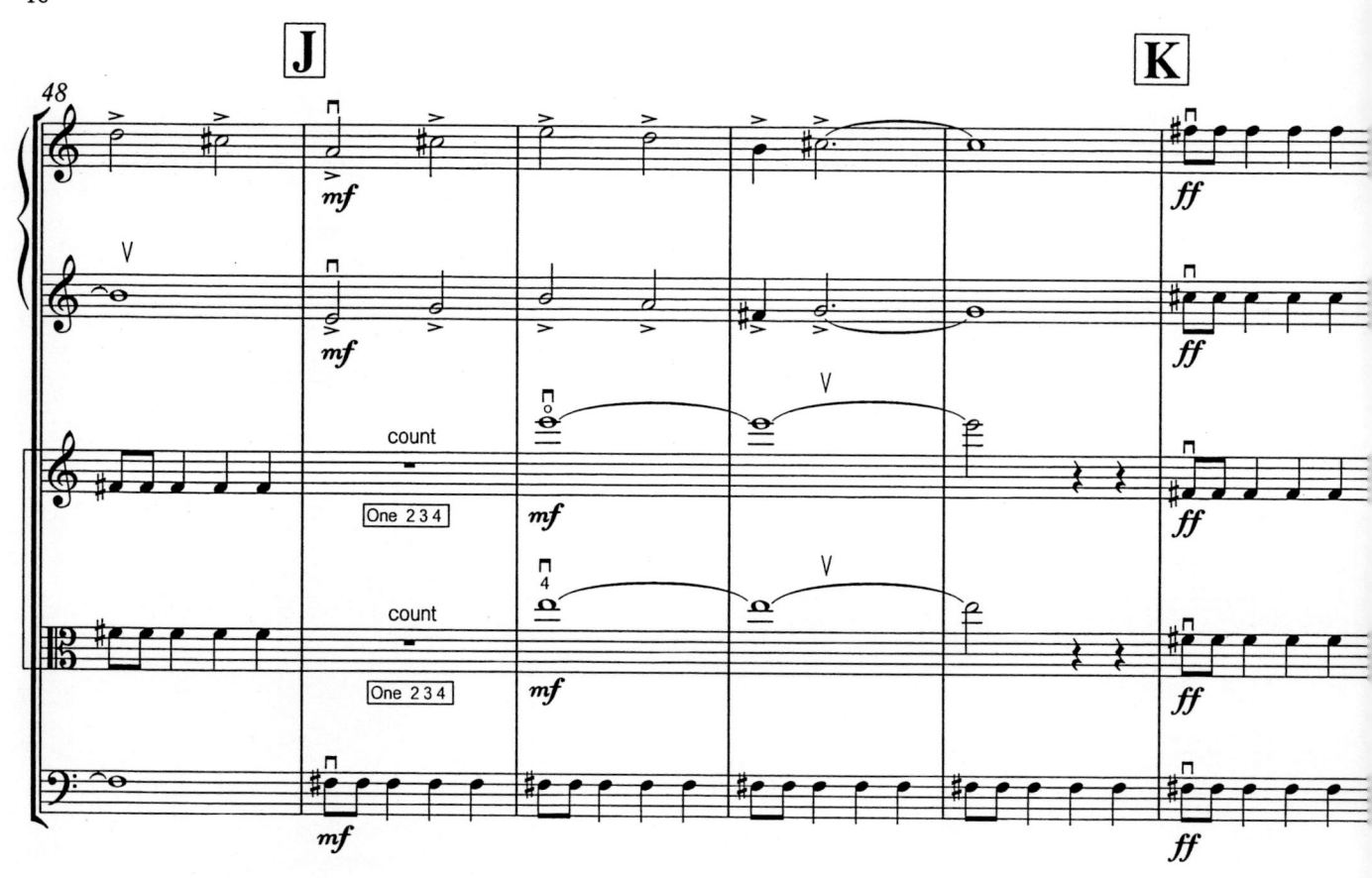

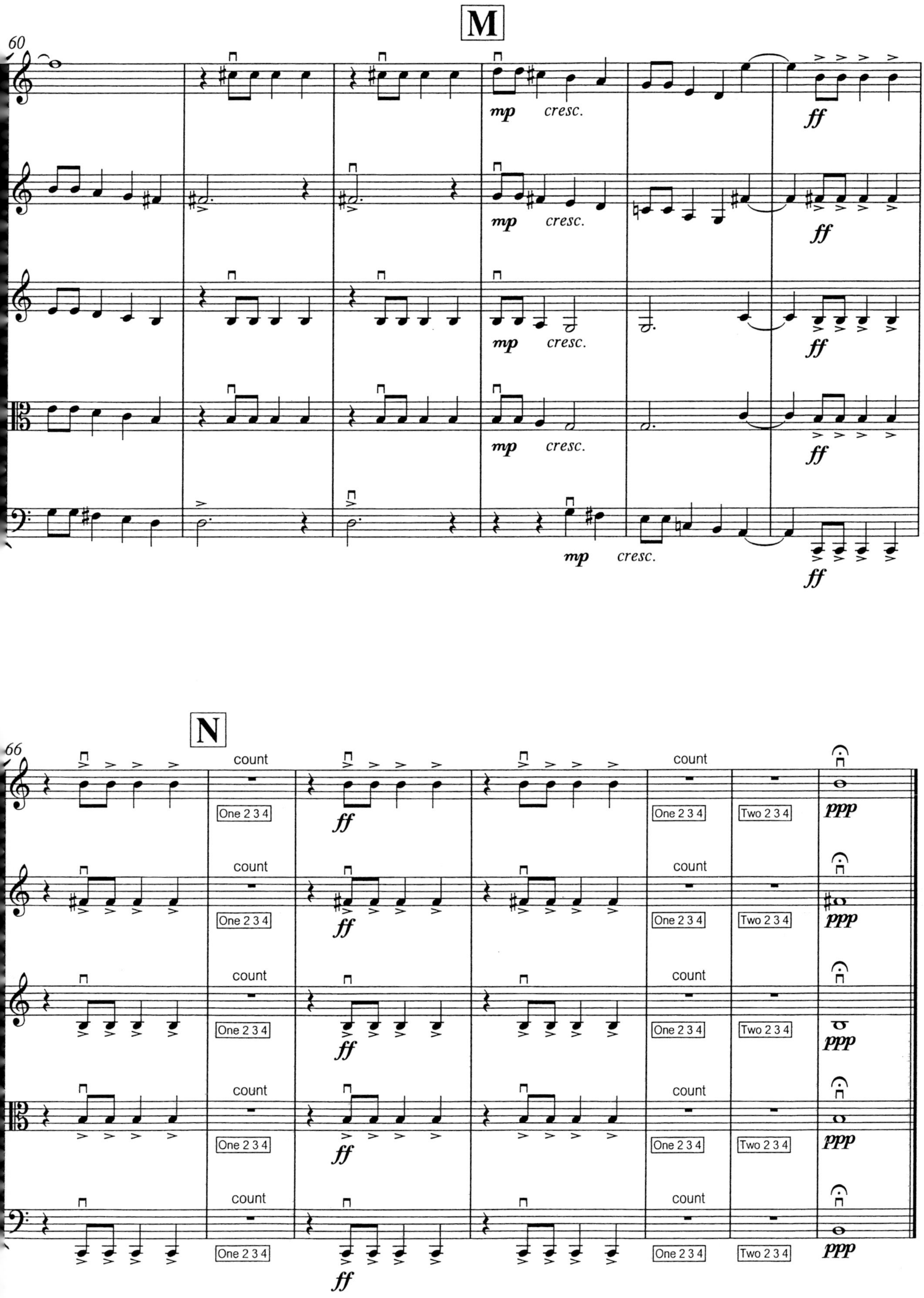
M
60
mp
cresc.
ff
N
66
count
One 2 3 4
Two 2 3 4
ppp

Alone on the Lake

Robert Spearing

REHEARSAL TIPS: Imagine the crotchet/quarter note figures are waves lapping gently; lighten the third crotchet/quarter note of each group. Players should feel a natural ebb and flow within an overall *pp* dynamic.

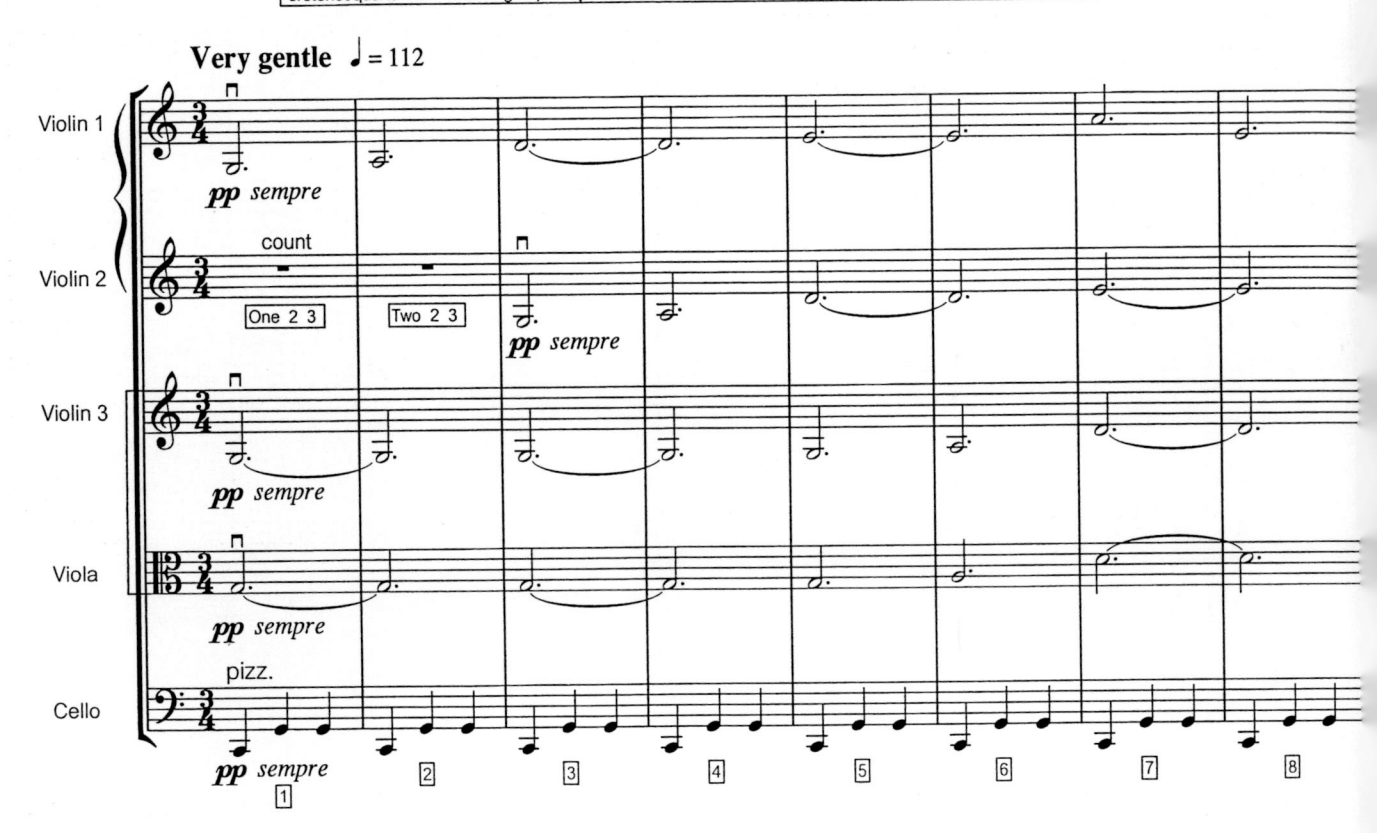

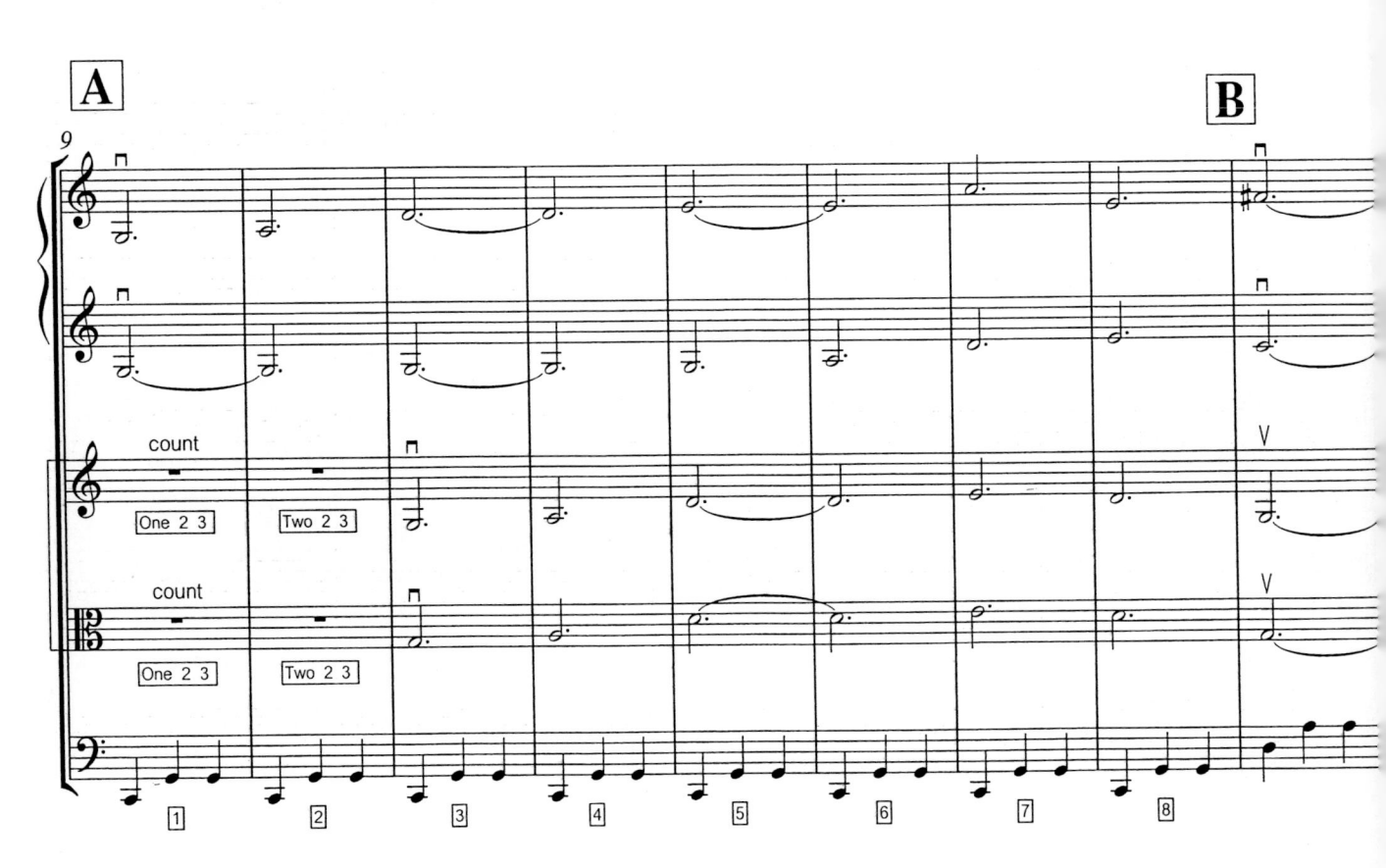

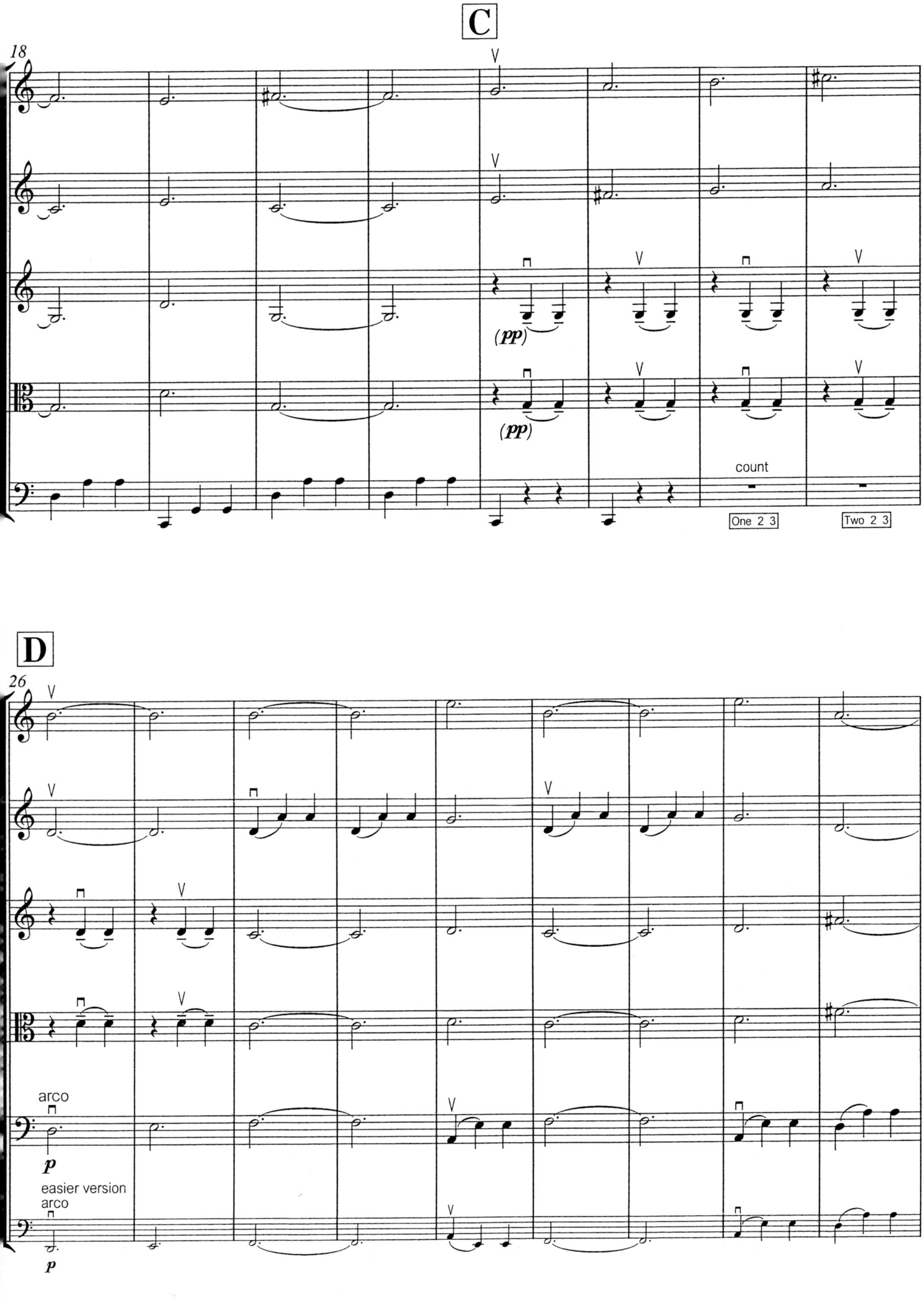
C
18
(pp)
(pp)
count
One 2 3
Two 2 3
D
26
arco
p
easier version
arco
p

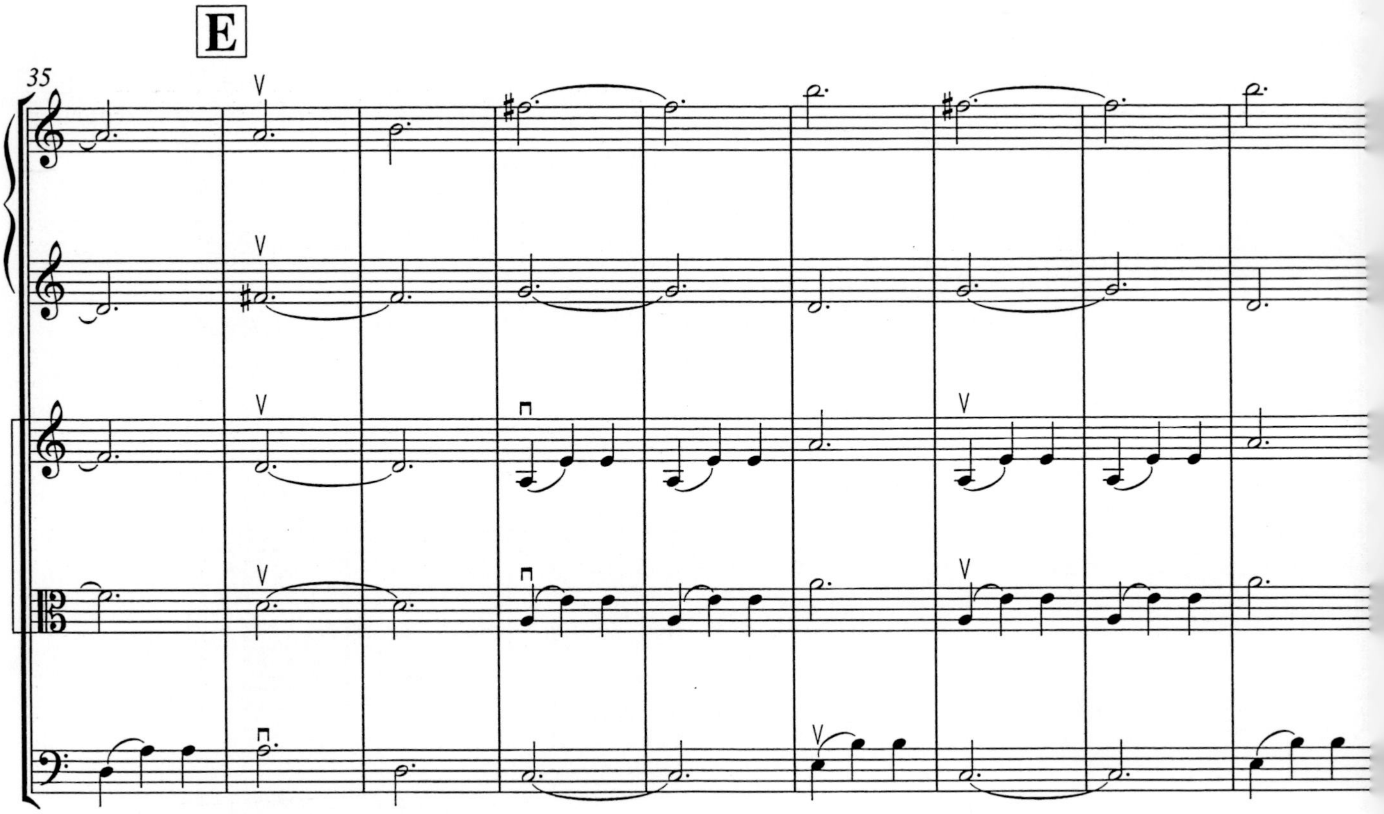
E
35

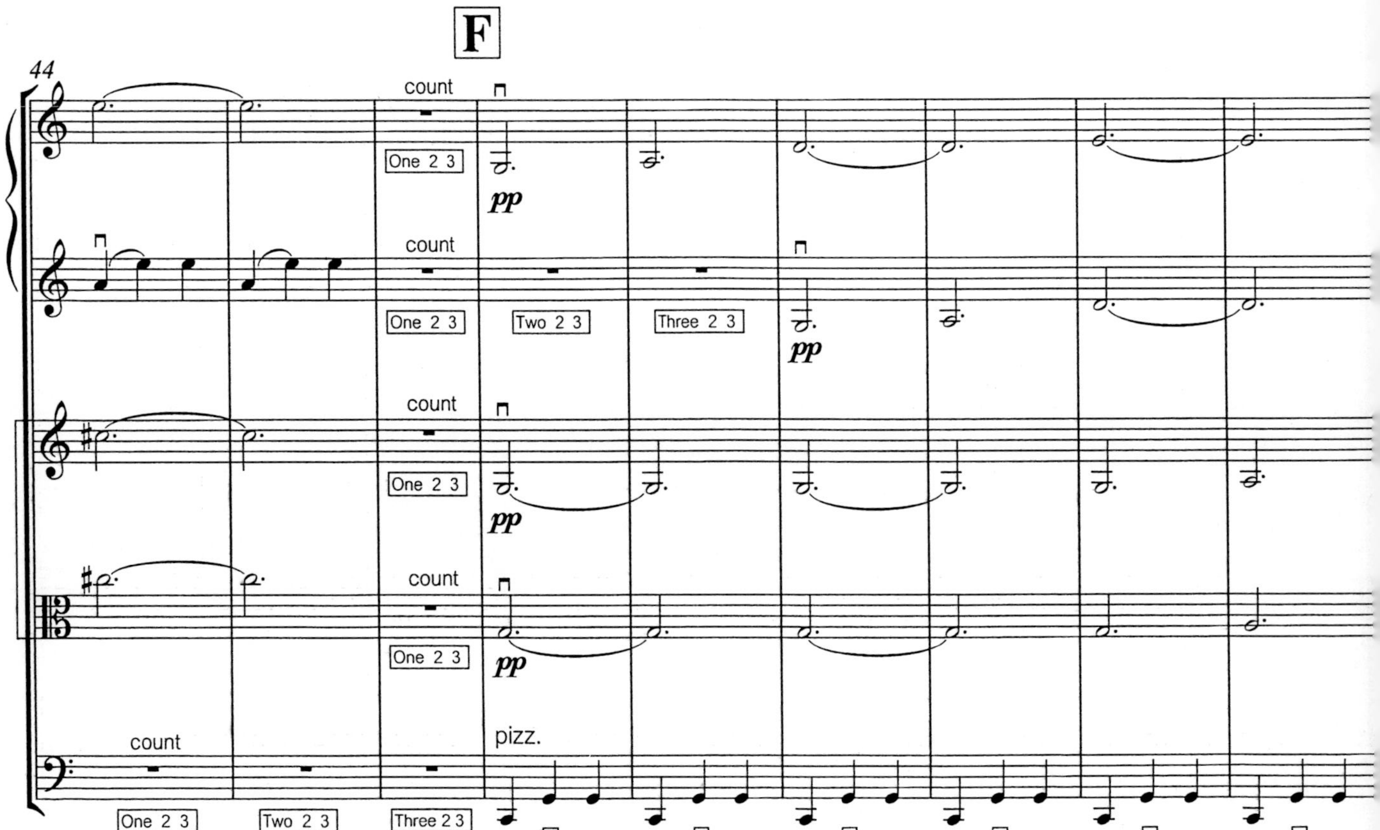
F
44
count
One 2 3
Two 2 3
Three 2 3
pp
pizz.
1
2
3
4
5
6

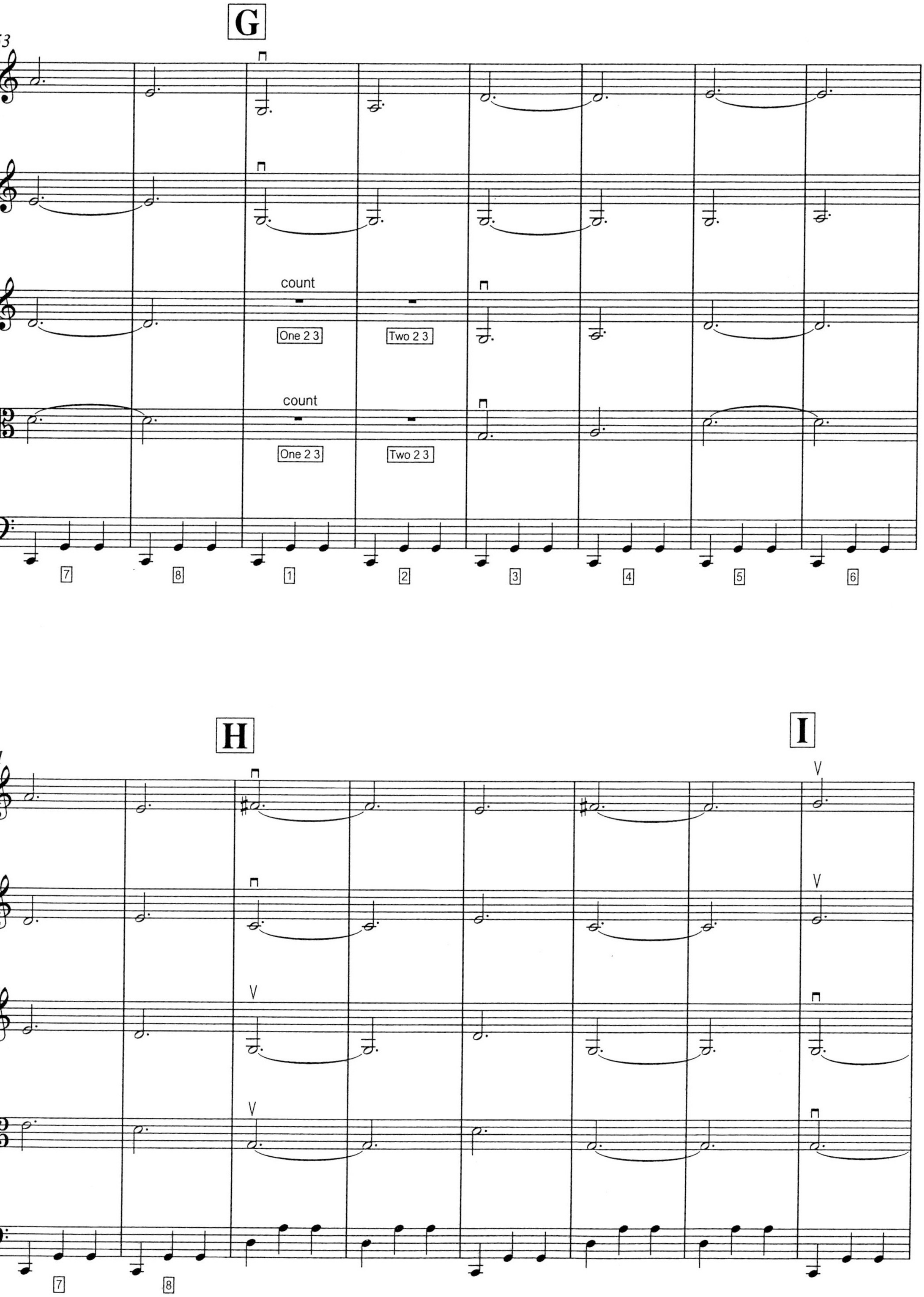
G
count
One 2 3
Two 2 3
count
One 2 3
Two 2 3
7
8
1
2
3
4
5
6
H
I
7
8

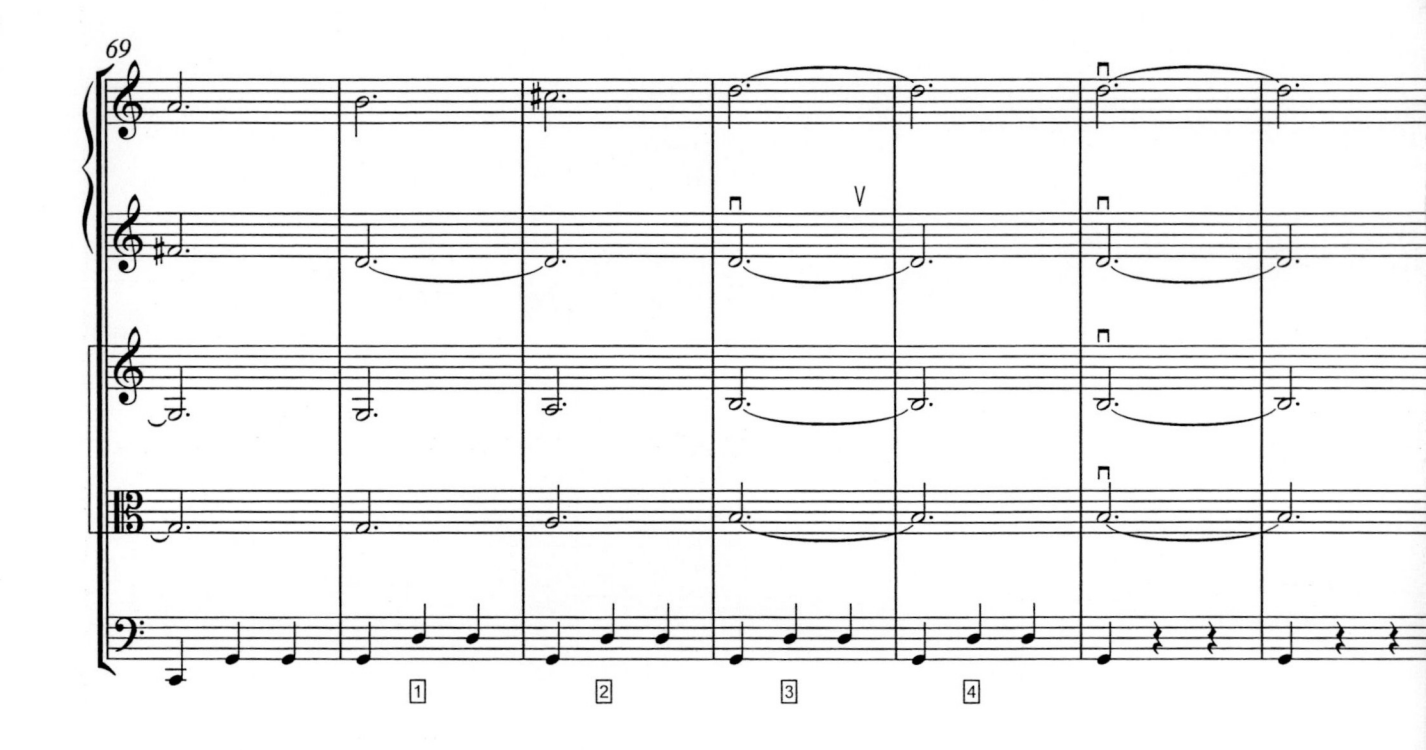

Chinese Street Festival
Drums and Dragons

Mary Cohen

REHEARSAL TIPS: At letters A, B and C everyone could watch the 1st violin for a fresh lead. It helps to practise looking back quickly from the *Dal Segno* instruction to the actual sign (at A).

B
stamp
col legno
mp
stamp
col legno
mp
stamp
col legno
mp
stamp
col legno
mp
stamp
arco
mf
1
stamp
FINE
stamp
stamp
stamp
stamp

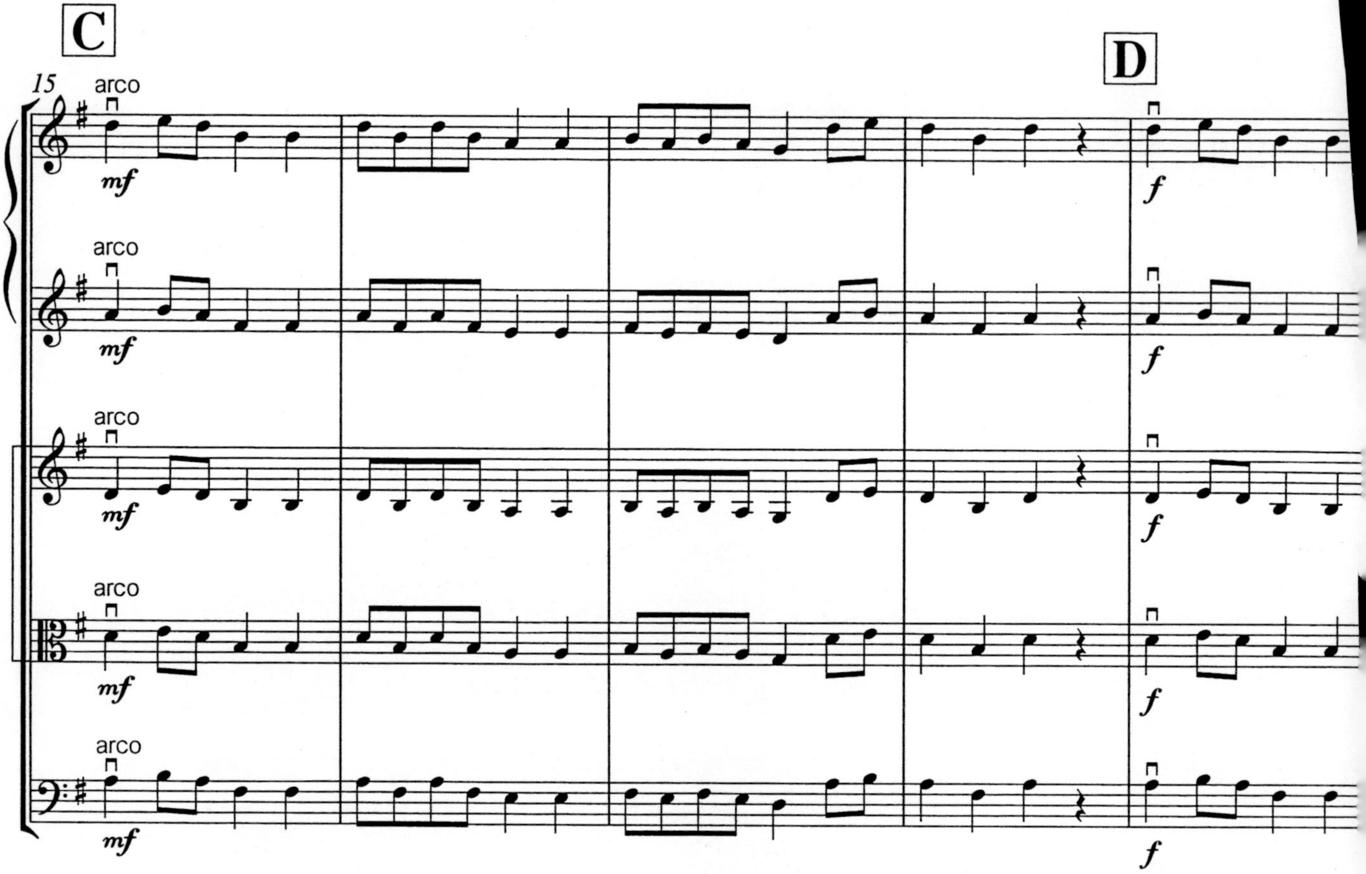
C
15
arco
mf
D
f

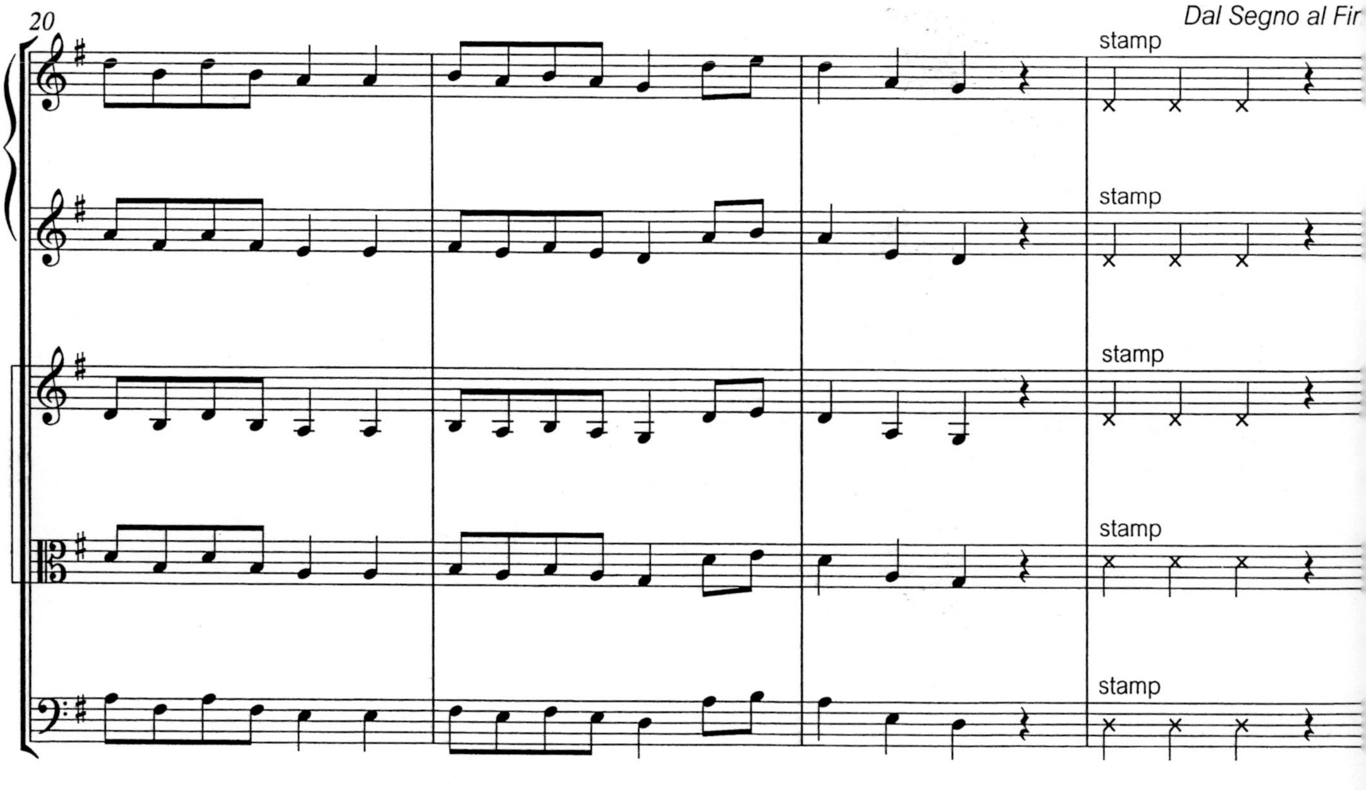
20
Dal Segno al Fir
stamp